Hello!

Most of the time I am a happy person, but there are a few things that I absolutely hate: lima beans, bullies, and moving. When I was a kid, I learned how to choke down lima beans (because my mother thought they were good for me) and how to stand up to bullies. But because of my father's job, we had to move every couple of years.

It was AWFUL.

The worst part was having to make new friends in school. I was a shy kid and meeting new people did not come easily to me. I always said exactly the wrong thing and felt like people were laughing at me. (They weren't!) That's why I identify so much with Jules in this book. She's struggling with the move and a new school and a busy family. But she finds comfort in animals, like so many of us. The question is, can she find a way to mend fences with Maggie and become a Vet Volunteer?

Enjoy!!

Laurie Halse Anderson

Collect All the Vet Volunteers Books

LAURIE HALSE ANDERSON

New Beginnings

PUFFIN BOOKS
An Imprint of Penguin Group (USA) Inc.

PUFFIN BOOKS
Published by the Penguin Group
Penguin Young Readers Group, 345 Hudson Street, New York, New York 10014, U.S.A.
Penguin Group (Canada), 90 Eglinton Avenue East, Suite 700, Toronto, Ontario, Canada M4P 2Y3
(a division of Pearson Penguin Canada Inc.)
Penguin Books Ltd, 80 Strand, London WC2R 0RL, England
Penguin Ireland, 25 St Stephen's Green, Dublin 2, Ireland (a division of Penguin Books Ltd)
Penguin Group (Australia), 250 Camberwell Road, Camberwell, Victoria 3124, Australia
(a division of Pearson Australia Group Pty Ltd)
Penguin Books India Pvt Ltd, 11 Community Centre, Panchsheel Park, New Delhi - 110 017, India
Penguin Group (NZ), 67 Apollo Drive, Rosedale, Auckland 0632, New Zealand
(a division of Pearson New Zealand Ltd)
Penguin Books (South Africa) (Pty) Ltd, 24 Sturdee Avenue, Rosebank, Johannesburg 2196, South Africa

Registered Offices: Penguin Books Ltd, 80 Strand, London WC2R 0RL, England

First published in the United States of America by Puffin Books,
a division of Penguin Young Readers Group, 2012

1 3 5 7 9 10 8 6 4 2

LIBRARY OF CONGRESS CATALOGING-IN-PUBLICATION DATA IS AVAILABLE

Puffin Books ISBN 978-0-14-241675-4

Text set in Joanna MT

Printed in the United States of America

PEARSON

For Lynn Hazen

Chapter One

●　●　●　●　●　●　●　●　●　●　●

The tabby cat with black, gray, and white stripes is hanging out near the Dumpster behind our store again. I've seen him every day since we moved here a week ago. It's getting late and I promised Mom I'd help with dinner, but I want to see if the cat's okay. Yesterday, he had a tear in his left ear, but he was too jittery to let me look at it closely or to clean it.

"Hey there, kitty," I say. "How's your ear? Still no tags or collar?"

"Meow," he says. He watches me, but keeps his distance, his ring-striped tail twitching from side to side. Aside from no collar or tag, and his ear, which looks like it's healing okay, he doesn't look like a stray. His coat is short, thick, and shiny, and he looks well fed. In fact, he's more chubby than sleek. Each day he comes a little closer to me and the water dish I set out for him, and twice he's let me pet him. I've been changing the water daily. Maybe today he'll let me pet him again and check his ear more closely.

"Meow?" he says again, this time a question.

"Yes, you can trust me," I say.

He tilts his head, and his green eyes stare right at me.

My twin brother, Josh, says I have a sixth sense—Animal Sense.

"I won't hurt you."

The tabby is still skittish, but he's so cute. I love his markings—gray, black, and white stripes, with two thicker black lines in his fur on the top of his head between his ears, forming what looks like a little M. He has more furry black V's accenting his eyes, and lots of fuzzy whiteness around his chin and neck. According to a cat website I found, he's a domestic shorthair brown mackerel tabby. But there is nothing common about him. His eyes and markings are so expressive. He's beautiful.

I kneel down a few feet behind the water dish and stay still. He finally approaches. He sniffs the water, laps at it, and then he walks closer to me.

I slowly lean forward, pausing before my hand reaches him. He sniffs it, and then rubs his furry forehead against my fingers. His slightly wet white whiskers tickle me as he tilts his head one way then another against my hand.

"Meow," he says again as I pet him, first his back, then his head, around his ears, including the ear with the little notch in it, and finally the warm, soft spot under his white chin until I feel and hear the vibration of his purr. Cats like me.

I miss petting the cats and kittens at the animal shelter back in Pittsburgh. This one reminds me of Moonshine, the orange tabby at the shelter. He was always a bit cautious, too. Before we moved here I volunteered there two days a week, helping clean up after the animals, washing their water and food dishes, petting and playing with the cats and kittens mostly, but sometimes the dogs and puppies, too. I helped get the animals socialized and friendly around people so they would have a better chance of being adopted.

"Where do you live?" I ask the tabby. "Do you have a home?"

He looks up at me as if he's about to tell me something important.

"Meow."

As soon as we get the hardware store Mom and

Dad bought all set up and open for business, I really want to volunteer at the shelter here in Ambler, too. I even got a recommendation letter from my supervisor back in Pittsburgh like Dad suggested. When the Ambler shelter sees my letter, I'm sure they'll let me volunteer.

The cat's purr gets louder and louder.

And I was excited to see that there's a veterinary clinic two blocks down the street. Maybe I'll make a copy of my letter to show the vets there, too. If I'm going to be a veterinarian someday, I have to get more experience, especially since we've never had any family pets of our own. Mom promised that we could finally get a pet once we'd settled in, but now she acts like it's the last thing on her mind.

Mom doesn't understand how much I love animals, how good I am with them, and how being around animals makes me less nervous. But Dad gets it. He's an animal lover, too. He loves to see them, pet them, and he talks to them, just like me. Mom is a worrier. She worries about germs, safety, and how expensive a pet might be. And she never seems to relax around animals or enjoy petting them like Dad and I do.

The tabby comes closer and circles me, leaning his body against my ankles and legs, then comes back around to my hands for more petting.

"I'd sure like to keep you," I say to him. "But you look like you already have a home. Still, you should be wearing a collar and a tag with your name and your owner's phone number on it." He's close to me again, purring and content.

The back door to the store creaks open and bangs against the wall, startling the cat and me. "Hey, Jules," Josh calls, "are you out here collecting strays again?" The cat sprints off across the back parking lot, out of sight.

"Josh!" I say. "You scared him away."

"Sorry," he says.

I look past the parking lot, hoping the tabby will come back, but he's gone. I hope his ear heals okay.

"Mom needs you upstairs," Josh says. "I'm helping Dad in the store. And Mom says we have to get ready for school tomorrow. I'm exhausted. So much for spring break!"

Josh is right. Spring break hasn't been a vacation this year. Sometimes, like right now, Josh and I think exactly alike. We have a six-year-old sister, Sophie, too, but Sophie and I rarely think alike. It must be because Josh and I are twins.

"The store's looking good, isn't it?" Josh asks.

"I guess so," I say.

I was excited when Mom and Dad bought the old boarded-up hardware store in Ambler. They renamed it Wrenches & Roses. Mom wants to add a bunch of gardening supplies and gift items to sell.

"Guess so? I know so," Josh says. "That sign you helped Dad build and paint looks great. The store still needs a lot of fixing up, but it's coming along."

Dad and I are handy with tools. Josh, not so much. He prefers to draw. Sophie draws, too. I like to build.

"I'm excited," Josh adds. "You should be, too."

"I'm excited about the store," I say. "I'm just not thrilled with the first day of school tomorrow. Or meeting new kids."

"It'll be fine," Josh says.

"I hope so." I shrug. "I'll be right in."

Josh heads in, and I hear him tromping up the stairs. Our apartment is above the store, and there's a huge basement below the store full of who knows what. Josh and I tried to explore down there the first day, but it was not on Mom's to-do list.

I look once more to see if the tabby is coming back. Nope. So I go inside, past the basement door, and head upstairs. Dad says the basement needs a lot of work so it's strictly "off limits" for now, though he promised we could add a family work-shop down there someday, where he could teach some do-it-yourself workshops about gardening techniques and home repairs for local families. There's a lot of room down there. And as he always says about everything, "There are so many possibilities."

Nothing is settled. Not in the basement, not in the store, and especially not in our apartment. There are boxes and packing materials everywhere.

"Jules, wash up and help me set the table," Mom says.

Sophie is in the living room, stacking empty boxes, open side out, one on top of the other. She makes a game of putting her stuffed animals in the boxes, talking to them as she goes. Poor kid. We need a real animal around here.

"Looking forward to going to school tomorrow?" Mom asks me.

"No, not really," I say.

I half expect Mom to start in again on her never-ending You're-in-Seventh-Grade-Now-Julia-So-Be-Sure-to-Stay-Organized-with-Your-Schoolwork speech, but instead she sighs and goes back to making dinner. She can't think of anything to say and neither can I. If I start telling her how I feel, I won't be able to stop. Plus, I don't think she is interested in how I feel.

"Get a good night's rest, Jules," Mom says. "It's

easier to start fresh when you've had a good night's sleep."

"Okay," I say.

"And don't forget to smile," she says. "It's a lot easier to meet new friends when you smile."

Mom makes it sound so easy. Why did she think moving to Ambler in March was such a great idea? If we had stayed in Pittsburgh for spring break, I could have worked the whole week at the shelter. Instead, Josh and I have been stuck packing, unpacking, and helping to set up Wrenches & Roses. The store opens in just two weeks.

Now spring break is over. Finished. Gone forever. And so are my Pittsburgh friends and the cats and dogs at the shelter there. I was getting good grades in my middle school back in Pittsburgh. School was fun, but that's because I knew everybody and everybody knew me.

After Mom and Dad both lost their jobs, they found the hardware store for sale. Since they had always dreamed of owning a small business, they said we couldn't pass up this opportunity, and I get that. But now Josh and I have to start all over again in a new school in a new town with only three months of the school year left. I won't know any of the kids, and they'll all have their own friends picked out already—ugh!

At least Josh will be with me tomorrow. I may be good with animals, but I am not very good at making friends. Josh usually helps with that, telling jokes, breaking the ice, introducing us, and answering all the twin questions. And there are always twin questions, usually really dumb questions like, "Are you identical twins?" Duh, hello, I'm a girl, he's a boy, so how could we be identical? Twins, yes. Identical, no. Josh always responds in a friendly way, explaining the difference between identical and fraternal twins.

Talking about being twins makes me nervous. Plus, most girls who ask about us being twins are just trying to get to know Josh, not me. I realize that I'm downright dreading starting at a new middle school. It's stressing me out. Whenever I felt stressed out back in Pittsburgh, I'd just pet the cats and dogs at the shelter, and that always calmed me down. But I haven't had a pet connection in two weeks, aside from the stray tabby in the alley, and he barely let me pet him.

I wish I could run away like the stray tabby, only I'd run all the way back to our old home and my old school and all my old friends.

Chapter Two

. . . .

Where's Dad?" I ask the next morning at breakfast.

"Dad went downstairs to the store early," Mom says. "He's expecting another big shipment today so he's getting the shelving ready. I expect you both to help out after school."

"I still wish Dad could drive us to school," I say. "At least on our first day."

"You'll be fine," Mom says. "The bus stop is right down the street. But you'd better hurry. You don't want to miss the bus!"

Of course Mom plans to take Sophie to first grade at her new elementary school. Sophie shouts from our room that she can't find her shoes.

"It's always something," Mom says.

Josh, hungry as usual, grabs another muffin and globs strawberry jam on it as Mom shoos us toward the door.

How can Josh be hungry at a time like this? I do not feel good about this day at all. Mom gives Josh and me each a kiss.

"Oh, wait," Mom says, reaching for a file folder.

"Mom—" I say, but she interrupts me.

"You'll both do great at your new school," Mom says. She takes a breath, as if trying to convince herself of what she's just said. "I've already registered you with the school secretary. They know you're coming. But she said she needed copies of your vaccination records and latest report cards." She holds up the folder, looking back and forth between Josh and me. "Don't worry, Jules," she says, "I have every confidence in you both." She hands the folder to Josh.

Mom seems to have more confidence in Josh than in me.

The kids at the bus stop nod when Josh says hi, but no one really talks to us. In fact, no one comes near us. Josh keeps smiling at everyone and making eye contact. He's good at playing the friendly guy. Not me.

Everyone pretty much avoids us except a red-haired girl with freckles carrying some kind of shoe box with a towel over the top. She walks past us as the bus pulls up. She stares at Josh's muffin and says, "You'd better hide that. The driver is a real grump about food on the bus."

The bus door opens, and everyone piles in. There is no garbage can inside or outside the bus, so Josh hands me Mom's folder, wraps the muffin in his paper towel, and hides it by cupping it between his hands.

"Take your seats!" the driver calls.

The red-haired girl pauses in front of me, trying to decide where to sit. There are only a few seats left. Both of her hands hold the box. She has no hands free to steady herself, so she turns around, facing me for a moment, and tries to back into the seat while holding the box with her two arms in front of her.

"Let me help," I say, reaching out, but that's when the bus jerks to a start, and I plow right into her. The box makes an awful crunching sound between us. "Sorry. Oh, I'm so sorry," I say, completely horrified, not just because of the box, but because my arms, neck, and face are right up against her chest; she's much taller than I am. My face is red hot, and I try to back up so I'm not so close. But the bus moves and I start to fall into her again.

"Watch it!" she yells as she angles her rear end into the seat.

"Take your seats!" the driver yells again.

Josh is right behind me, and when he falls forward into me, he pushes me into the seat beside her. Even worse, his muffin flies up in the air. I can't believe this is happening. I drop the folder and try to catch the jam-covered muffin. But I miss it, and it goes right past me, skimming the edge of the red-haired girl's towel and cardboard box. The muffin disappears near our feet. I'm hoping it didn't land on the file folder.

The girl beside me is still and silent. The word *livid* from last year's spelling bee comes to mind. I can't make myself look at her, so I look at Josh instead. He found a spot to sit across from me, one seat back.

When the girl beside me leans over her shoe box to look at her feet, the box buckles even more. I look, too. Josh's upside-down muffin on the floor would be bad enough. But this is worse. It missed the file folder, but it's upside down on her sneaker.

"Oh," I say, grabbing the file folder and stuffing the now-wrinkled papers back into it. "I'm so sorry. Sorry, sorry, sorry. It was an accident."

She gasps. There's a brief moment of silence before she yells, "You ruined everything!"

Okay, this is bad, but it's just a shoe. I don't know why she is freaking out.

"Sorry," Josh says. He tries to hand her the paper towel he is still holding, even though it's covered in jam from the muffin.

"Get away! Both of you, just get away!"

"Don't yell at my brother," I say. "You can wash your sneaker."

"I don't care about my shoe. Look what you did to my science project! I've been working on it for weeks. You crushed it!"

The bus driver looks at us in his rearview mirror. In fact, I'm sure everyone on the bus is looking at us. I bet my face is as red as the strawberry jam.

Another girl behind us peeks over and under the seat, then she asks the redhead, "Are those the sneakers your cousin sent you from Hollywood?"

"Yeah," the redhead says.

Hollywood? Please, who buys their shoes in Hollywood? Who does she think she is?

"Come to my locker when we get to school," the other girl says. "I have an extra pair of sneakers."

"Thanks," the redhead says, loud enough for the whole bus to hear. "What I'm going to need is glue and a whole new science project. If I get a bad grade, I'll be grounded for life. "

Josh leans toward her and turns on his charm. Once more he says, "We're really sorry—"

"Don't talk to me," the redhead says, lifting the towel and peeking at her project. Then she tries to kick the muffin onto my shoes.

Josh convinces the kid next to him to move back a row when the driver isn't looking.

"Jules," he says, motioning to the empty spot next to him.

Josh and I slump in tandem beside each other.

"Well, things can only get better now," Josh whispers to me, trying to make me smile.

"Yeah," I say.

I hate that we have to start all over again in a new middle school. I hate riding the school bus. I hate that girl. And it's pretty clear that she hates me, too.

Chapter Three

· · · · · · · · · · · ·

We find the office. At least the school secretary welcomes us.

"Just in time," she says. "Principal Phillips was just heading out. Mr. Phillips, these are our new students I told you about, Julia and Joshua Darrow."

"Hello, hello," the principal says. "Great to have you here. Sorry to rush off, but we've got an overflowing water fountain and a miniflood in the gym." Then he hurries out the door.

Two students about our age come in, and the secretary introduces us to David Hutchinson, who will be Josh's school buddy for the day, and Sunita Patel, who will show me around. Josh and I briefly compare schedules, but we have no classes together. I was afraid of that. The trouble is, twins aren't usually put together in the same classes. Mom says it's because separating twins helps them become independent. So I'll be on my own, except for lunch.

I wait for Josh to say something first. His friendly personality usually puts everyone at ease, including me. But after the whole school bus fiasco, he's quieter than usual.

David asks, "Where are you from?"

"Pittsburgh," Josh answers. But that's it. He doesn't say more than that.

Our morning didn't get off to a great start, but David and Sunita seem nice. Sunita is pretty with long black hair and a friendly smile. She rolls her eyes as David jokes about "making pit stops in Pittsburgh." David has a loud voice, just like my little sister, Sophie. Josh smiles. Once Josh starts feeling better, they'll get along just great.

The bell rings. "See you at lunch," I tell Josh.

But as we walk down the hall, Sunita looks at my schedule and says, "We have alternating lunch periods here. You might or might not see your brother at lunchtime."

"Oh," I say.

Sunita must sense the dread in my voice. She looks right at me.

"Don't worry," she says.

"I can't help it," I say. "I'm not good at meeting new people."

"Just think positive," Sunita says. "Besides, I've got the same lunch period as you, so look for me if you don't see Josh. And really, everyone is so friendly here, you'll make lots of friends right away, I'm sure."

Everyone is so friendly? Clearly she doesn't know the mean red-headed girl from the bus. I'm about to say something, but Sunita locks elbows with me and says, "Hurry, now."

She steers me through the crowded halls, upstairs to Room 202. "You have Mr. Hart, the same science teacher I had last year. You're going to love his class!"

I bet Sunita is one of those people who never feels lost and always knows what to do and say. I'm one of those people who never knows what to say, so I say nothing. Then people think I'm a snob. Or if I do say something, half the time I blurt out the wrong thing and embarrass myself.

Sunita is right about Mr. Hart. His science room is filled with animals. Live animals. Lots of them—a corn snake, a bearded dragon lizard, a tarantula, and the most adorable lop-eared rabbit I have ever seen. The rabbit is small, and that makes its big floppy ears hanging down all the sweeter.

Sunita introduces me to Mr. Hart, and he points me to an empty chair near the rabbit. She walks me all the way to my desk, then whispers, "We'll talk after class. I gotta run, but I'll be back to guide you to all your classes through lunch."

"Thanks," I say.

Sunita's positive attitude must be rubbing off on me. Plus, I feel ten times more relaxed being around all of Mr. Hart's animals. I'm so close to the bunny, I can't help smiling. Things are looking up.

I sit in the empty chair next to the furry little rabbit. She must be a dwarf. She's hopping, then hiding under a little basket. She pokes her cute nose out from under the basket and sniffs the air, wiggling her whiskers. She tilts her head and looks right at me. I can't wait to pet her.

"Welcome back, everybody. We have a new student today who has just moved to Ambler. Please welcome your new classmate, Julia," Mr. Hart says.

"Jules," I say.

Everyone turns to stare at me. A few kids nod and smile, but I avoid their eyes by looking at the rabbit.

"Okay, then. Welcome, Jules," Mr. Hart says. "Now, our first order of business today is to review the science tests you took before spring break."

He hands back the tests to some groans from the class. Of course I don't have a test, but he tells me to look on with the girl across the aisle from me. She halfheartedly moves her desk closer to mine, but then she starts doodling on her paper. I don't blame her.

Mr. Hart drones on and on about the importance of rocks, sediments, and fossils. I try to listen at first, but I'm having a hard time paying attention. I can't stop looking at the dwarf rabbit with her long, floppy ears. The tiny V of her mouth is surrounded by the softest-looking brown and white fur and the most adorable little bunny chin. She's out from under her basket and sniffing around the cage. I wish I had a carrot or something to feed her.

I reach through the wire cage with my fingers. Curious, she hops closer and sniffs me. Her whiskers tickle and I can't help smiling, but I hold my fingers still. She tilts her head, and I stroke the spot on the top of her head between her ears. She leans closer to my hand and now I can reach her velvety ears, warm and soft. The grid of the cage is too small to reach my hand all the way through to pet her. I study the latch on the front of the cage to see if I can open it quietly. Mr. Hart is still lecturing about geologic processes.

I open the little hook very slowly so I won't scare the bunny and so the hook won't make any noise. She hops away when I reach in, but when I hold my hand still, she comes back toward me. She lets me pet her soft fur, first on her head and ears again, then down her back. I want to take her out of her cage and put her on my lap. School would be so much easier if we could bring our own pets. That's what I'm thinking when I realize Mr. Hart isn't talking anymore. No one is talking or doing anything because everyone, including Mr. Hart, is staring at me.

Uh-oh. Now what have I done?

I slowly pull my hand out of the cage. "Sorry," I say. I latch the catch securely.

"Wow," says the girl across the aisle. "Chewie let you pet her?"

"Chewie?" I ask.

"Yeah, Chewie. That's her name." She points to the bunny.

"She didn't try to bite you?" another kid asks.

"No, why?" I ask.

"It appears we have a bunny whisperer among us," Mr. Hart announces.

Several students laugh.

"All I did was pet her," I say.

"Yes, but no one has been able to pet her since

we got her two months ago. She bites and scratches and is a bit of a nervous Nellie. You're the first
person, as far as we know, who she's let pet her."

"Oh," I say. I look at Chewie and she looks back
at me, cute and innocent.

"Do you have rabbits or other pets at home?"
Mr. Hart asks.

My face warms. "No," I say. "But I volunteered
at the animal shelter in Pittsburgh. I'm very good
with animals."

"I can see that," Mr. Hart says, rubbing his chin.
"Chewie needs a new home. She isn't getting along
with the students. Maybe you'd like to give it a
try."

"That'd be great," I say.

"You'll need your parents' permission of course."

"I'm sure my parents will agree," I say. What am
I thinking? Dad might agree. But Mom? I'll need
all the help I can get to convince her. I have to talk
to Josh as soon as possible.

"All right, Jules from Pittsburgh," Mr. Hart
says, "please see me after class. We'll discuss the
details."

Mr. Hart begins to make another announcement
about some kind of upcoming streams cleanup
event, but I'm having a hard time paying attention.
I can't stop smiling and looking at Chewie, who

has one ear up and one ear down. She looks like she is smiling, too. It's a goofy little smile, with her front teeth sticking out just a tiny bit.

Finally I'll have a pet to care for. I start thinking about building Chewie a bigger home than the little cage she's in now. This cage might be good for carrying her safely from one place to another and maybe for sleeping at night. But I learned at the Pittsburgh shelter that all animals, including rabbits, need enough space to run or hop around and play. I'll make her a tunnel, agility ramps, and hidey holes, too.

Science class zips by. The more I think about having Chewie as a pet, the more excited I get. The morning that started out so badly is definitely looking up.

Chapter Four

. . . .

Sunita is right there after science class, and she stays with me while I talk to Mr. Hart. Sunita smiles and gives me a thumbs-up when she hears I'm going to bring Chewie home. She's so nice, and she looks truly happy for me.

"You're lucky it's a cute bunny that needs a home," Sunita says. "Last summer, Mr. Hart was looking for someone to take care of the class snake!"

Mr. Hart chuckles and hands me a folder about rabbit care. He tells me I need a letter from my parents giving their permission and saying that we all understand what's required to be a responsible pet owner of Chewie. I'm worried about Mom agreeing. What if she says we don't have any extra money for pet supplies?

Then Mr. Hart says, "Tell your parents that if this works out long term, you can have the cage, litter box, and water bottle, too."

"Thank you, Mr. Hart. Thank you!" I say. I can't wait to tell Josh.

"I have to warn you," Mr. Hart says. "Several students before you have taken Chewie home, and unfortunately those trials all ended in disaster. She's not the tamest of bunnies. I see you have a way with animals, and that's great. But this is more or less Chewie's last chance with us. If it doesn't work out, she might need to go to a rabbit rescue foster home."

"I'm sure it will work," I say as the kids in Mr. Hart's next class start filing in. "I helped socialize lots of cats when I volunteered at the shelter in Pittsburgh."

"Okay, then," Mr. Hart says. "Bring me a note from your parents and we'll let you do your bunny whisperer magic."

Sunita and I laugh about my being a bunny whisperer as she pulls me quickly through the hall to my next class, which is language arts.

"I'm so excited for you," Sunita says. "Chewie is adorable. Are you sure your mom and dad will let you adopt her?"

"Yes," I say. "They promised we could get a pet once we were settled. And with a free cage and all, I'm sure they'll agree. Plus, Josh is very convincing. They always listen to him. Hopefully I can talk to Josh at lunch and we can call home. My parents know I'm good with animals. Maybe my mom will write the permission note today and pick Chewie up with us at the end of the day. Otherwise, tomorrow, for sure."

"That's great," Sunita says. "It took me forever to convince my mom to let me adopt a cat. But she finally agreed."

"You have a cat? Oh, I love cats! You're so lucky. I wish I had a cat, too."

"Yes, her name is Mittens."

My language arts teacher is talking to a couple of students in the hall when we reach my classroom, so Sunita stays and sits with me at an empty table in the back. "I'd like to meet Mittens," I say to Sunita. "What does she look like?"

"She's a black tuxedo cat with white paws. You'll have to come over someday to see her. Did you really volunteer at the shelter?"

I nod.

"Then we have a lot in common," Sunita says. "I have twins in my family, too. They're only five, but they're fraternal twins, like you and your brother. My brother's name is Harshil and my sister is Jasmine."

Sunita understands twins! "I have a little sister, too," I say. "Sophie is six. What else do we have in common?"

"Well," Sunita says. "I volunteer also. At the local veterinary clinic—Dr. Mac's Place. A bunch of us help with cleaning up and caring for the animals there. David does, too."

"Wow, I'd love to do something like that," I say. "Could you introduce me to Dr. Mac?"

"Sure," Sunita says. "But I can do better than that. I'll introduce you to Maggie. Dr. Mac is Maggie's grandmother. Maggie lives with Dr. Mac right there at the clinic. Maggie is super nice and goes to school here. All the Vet Volunteers are great."

"Wow, Vet Volunteers. How many of you are there?"

"Five of us usually—Maggie, David, Zoe, Brenna, and me. And sometimes, if it's really busy, a younger girl named Taryn helps out. I'm not sure if Dr. Mac has room for more, but we can ask. Sometimes Zoe is out of town staying with her mom, and David is busy at the horse stables. Let's ask Maggie and see what she thinks."

I can't wait to meet Maggie, and to tell Josh about Chewie. Once we convince Mom and Dad to adopt our very own rabbit, Ambler might not be so bad after all. Plus, if I have a pet of my own, I'll be able to show Dr. Mac how good I am with animals.

"May I see the bunny facts?" Sunita asks.

"Sure," I say, opening the folder Mr. Hart gave me.

Sunita smiles and points to the cute pictures of bunnies grooming themselves and using the litter box. "Just like Mittens," she says.

We read about how friendly, social, and smart rabbits are and the way they like to be petted.

"Oh, I didn't know rabbits don't usually like to be picked up or held on your lap," I say.

"Me neither," Sunita says. "Looks like rabbits have different personalities, too. It says some are shy, some friendly, some calm, some nervous, some playful and curious."

I don't say it out loud but I think that if I were a rabbit, I'd be the shy, nervous type. Josh, of course, would be the friendly bunny.

"Chewie seems friendly and outgoing. I don't know why everyone is so afraid of her," I say.

"You should have seen her in class. She kept poking her nose through the bars of the cage, standing on her hind feet, and begging me to pet her. She's so alert and curious. And clean. She's so cute the way she washes one ear at a time with both of her paws."

"Sweet," Sunita says. "Uh-oh, did you see this?" She points to a paragraph in bold type about how rabbits like to chew on everything, including furniture and electric cords.

Uh-oh is right. Mom will not like that.

"Maybe that's why she's named Chewie?" Sunita says. "Oops, gotta go now."

My teacher finally comes in and assigns me to an empty desk. Sunita waves to me from the door and mouths, "See you later."

My teacher leads a discussion about a book I have already read. She asks questions, and I know the answers. But I don't know any of the kids in the class. I keep my hand down and my eyes on my desk so she won't call on me. I'm still the shy, nervous bunny.

During silent reading, the teacher suggests I pick a book from the back of the room. I nod and pick one, but I have a hard time focusing. Instead, I think about Chewie and how fun it'll be to have her as my very own pet. I pull out my notebook and start a list of ways to convince Mom to let me keep Chewie.

I'll have to think of a way to keep Mom and Dad's furniture safe from Chewie, and Chewie safe from any electrical cord danger. I'll build a bunny-proof environment for her. I draw a simple sketch of the room I share with Sophie and where Chewie's cage and play area will be. There is also a coupon in the folder for Chewie to be spayed at Dr. Mac's when she is old enough. I wonder how old she is now. I'll have to ask Mr. Hart.

The rest of the morning goes great, until lunch, that is. The cafeteria food is bland. The pizza has no flavor, and the carrots have no crunch. The only good thing about lunch is Sunita. She shares some of her homemade lentils. They are spicy but good. Mom used to have time to make our lunches. Not anymore. I don't see Josh anywhere, so Sunita was right. Josh and I are scheduled for different times on the alternating lunch period. Sunita looks around, but she can't find Maggie, either. Lunch is almost over.

"If Maggie is in any of your afternoon classes, maybe you can tell her about me," I say to Sunita as we finish our lunches.

"Wait, let me see your schedule again," Sunita says. "The only class Maggie and I are in together is gym, but we don't have it today. Gym meets every other day. Maggie and I are on the Tuesday-Thursday block schedule for gym. And team sports meet every day after school, too. Maggie's a great athlete. She's on the basketball team. Do you play team sports?"

"Not me," I say, and hand my schedule to Sunita. "Block scheduling is kind of confusing."

"Don't worry, it'll make sense soon. My first week here I was completely lost. You're doing great." Sunita studies my schedule again. I'm glad she understands. "At Ambler, the girls and boys have separate gym classes, but the classes are mixed with kids from all the grades," she explains. "Great, look—you're on the same Tuesday-Thursday gym schedule as Maggie and me! So I can introduce you tomorrow afternoon for sure."

"Thanks," I say, but I'm disappointed I won't meet Maggie today.

Sunita smiles and says, "And there is only one Maggie in the whole school. So if you see or hear someone talking to a Maggie, that'll be her. Just introduce yourself. She's great."

I hope I'll have the courage to talk to Maggie on my own. She sounds like someone I'd really like to have as a friend.

Chapter Five

. . . .

After lunch, Sunita walks with me up the super-crowded stairway to my study skills class on the third floor.

"What luck," Sunita says. "There she is!" She grabs my arm and pulls me through the crowd.

"Excuse me, excuse me," Sunita says as we weave our way up the stairs.

I'm excited, but it's so crowded that I can't figure out which girl is Maggie.

Uh-oh, I see the mean red-haired girl from the bus ahead of us. I let go of Sunita and go slower, hanging back, hoping that the red-haired girl will keep going and not notice me. Sunita waves to someone.

"Maggie, wait up!" Sunita calls out.

The red-haired girl stops and turns around.

Oh no. My heart sinks.

This couldn't possibly be Sunita's friend Maggie. But Sunita said there was only one Maggie in the whole school. So it must be the one and only Maggie, whose grandma is the veterinarian.

Yep, it's her.

Maggie gives me a look, but waits for us to catch up in the hall at the top of the stairs. I know I should say something, but we already got off to such a bad start I'm worried that I might make it worse.

Luckily, Sunita jumps in and starts talking. "This is Jules," she says to Maggie. "She and her family just moved here. I'm her school buddy today."

Sunita turns to me and says, "Maggie's grandmother is Dr. Mac—she runs the veterinary clinic."

"Um, we sort of met," I start, not knowing what to say. "I kind of accidentally ruined her science project on the bus this morning." I turn to Maggie. "I'm Jules. And I'm still sorry."

"Hi," Maggie replies. She doesn't seem happy to be talking to me, but she's not yelling at me, either.

"Will you be at the clinic after school today?"

Sunita asks her. "Dr. Mac asked me to come in and help feed the abandoned kittens."

"Those kittens are cute, but man, do they need a lot of attention!" Maggie says, smiling. "But I'm not on kitten duty today. I have tutoring and then basketball practice, so I won't be home until dinnertime."

"You're a tutor?" I ask hurriedly. Maybe this is a chance for me to connect with Maggie on something. "That's cool. Sometimes I help my little sister, Sophie, with her homework. Maybe I could be a tutor, too." I'm about to ask Maggie more about it, but she's giving me a not-so-friendly look.

"I *have* a tutor," Maggie says. "Not that it's any of your business." All traces of her smile are totally gone now. "See you later, Sunita," she says, walking off.

I don't know what to say. Having a tutor is nothing to be embarrassed or mad about, but once again I've stumbled into making Maggie mad at me. How could this keep happening? And how am I going to fix it?

I don't feel like talking much after that. Sunita is still friendly. She says, "I'm glad you and Maggie have met," but she doesn't say anything more about my chances of being a Vet Volunteer.

A few minutes later, Sunita and I arrive at room

307. I'm feeling lousy about messing up with Maggie again and am not really looking forward to a whole new class full of students I don't know. I say good-bye to Sunita, take a deep breath, and open the door.

Everyone in the class turns to look at me.

The study skills teacher smiles, and tells me her name is Ms. Harris. "You must be Julia. Come on in," she says. She asks if I want to say something about myself.

"No, not really. Although I prefer to be called Jules. Thanks," I say, staying near the door.

"Please allow me to introduce you," Ms. Harris says. "Class, this is Jules Darrow."

A few of the kids smile at me.

"Jules," the teacher says, "I usually have my new students fill out this survey for me."

"What kind of survey?" I ask.

The teacher smiles again and holds out a packet of papers toward me. "It's to help determine your unique learning style," she says. "So I can help you utilize the best study strategies."

"Can I take it home to do it?" I ask.

Ms. Harris laughs, but it's not a mean laugh. "It will only take you a few minutes. And it's nothing to worry about. There are no right or wrong answers. You can fill it out here in the classroom, or if you want, you can use the desk in the hallway. Your fellow students will be practicing their oral reports in a moment, so that might be distracting."

She walks closer to me and hands me the stapled papers. The rest of the class waits silently and stares at me. I look at the survey and wish I could disappear. I hate being the new kid.

The teacher whispers, but of course everyone hears her when she asks me, "Do you need some help getting started?"

I take a breath and look at my shoes. "I don't need any help," I say quietly.

"Do you have a pen or pencil?"

I feel trapped in this room, just like the poor dogs at the shelter in Pittsburgh, pacing endlessly back and forth in their cages. I take a step toward the doorway. "I have a pen. I'll take the test in the hall, thanks." It comes out more rushed than I planned, but I can't wait to get out of there. Why is meeting new people so hard for me?

The next few minutes I sit in the hall checking off boxes with *always, sometimes, often, rarely,* and *never.*

It basically comes down to this:

I can answer *sometimes* for almost everything. *Sometimes* I like meeting new people. Especially new people like Sunita, who are friendly and put me at ease. Otherwise, *rarely. Sometimes* I like working with others, but *usually* it takes me a few weeks to feel comfortable. But I can't write all that down. I have to check one of the boxes instead.

For all the questions about doing schoolwork independently and on time, I check off *usually.* I don't want Ms. Harris to think I'm not a good student. I am.

Too bad there are no questions about under-standing, helping, and being good with animals. That's something I could check *always* for. I browse my answers and look around the empty hallway. I don't want to be sitting out here when the bell rings. Finally I return to the classroom and turn my paper in to Ms. Harris. Even though she said there are no right or wrong answers, I wonder what she'll think about me. Honestly, I think my study skills are just fine. It's my people skills I keep messing up with. But again, there's no box on the survey to check off for that.

Chapter Six

• • • • • • • • • • • •

After my study skills class, I see Josh in the hall, putting books in his locker.

"Hey, Jules, just two more classes then we're done. How's your day going?"

"It started great. The science teacher said I could adopt Chewie."

"Chewie?"

"Chewie's a rabbit," I say. "And you have to help me convince Mom and Dad we can adopt her."

"You mean like take it home and keep it as a family pet forever?"

"Yeah, cool, right? Mom and Dad said we could get a pet once we settled in."

"Yeah, but a rabbit? I wanted a dog."

"They are more likely to agree to a rabbit," I say. "Rabbits are easier to take care of and cheaper, too. You should see her. She's adorable. Then in a few months we'll start working on Mom and Dad about getting a puppy. They'd never agree to a puppy now, with the store opening in two weeks. Puppies are a lot of work."

"True," Josh says, slamming his locker shut. "But you better think of a new name for your rabbit, something that sounds tame and sweet and well behaved. Believe me, 'Chewie' is not it. Do you really think Mom will allow any animal in the house with that name?"

"No," I sigh. "You're right."

Josh checks his watch and his schedule, then says, "Hey, David told me about a group of kids called Vet Volunteers—they help a veterinarian down the street from us."

"Yeah, Sunita told me about them, too. There's only one problem. You know that red-haired girl who freaked out on the bus this morning?"

Josh nods.

"Well, that's Maggie. And Dr. Mac, the veterinarian, is her grandmother. Plus, wait till you hear what happened in the hallway when I saw her again. I'm sure Maggie hates me now."

"What happened?"

I tell him about the tutoring mix-up. "Maggie took it the wrong way, and I'm sure she thinks I was trying to insult her."

Josh shakes his head.

"Josh, you've got to help me smooth things over."

He looks me right in the eye. "Look, Jules, why don't you try being friendly for a change? Maybe even smile now and then?" he says. "I can't go on fixing all your problems. You messed up, Jules, so you fix it. I'm going to class."

Josh disappears down the hall.

Fix it with Maggie? Sure. How am I supposed to do that?

I walk to my next class, and that's when I see Maggie in the hall, talking to Mr. Hart, my science teacher. He's got his hands on his hips and is shaking his head. Maggie is holding the shoe box I bumped into on the bus. My math class is just beyond them, so there is no way around. Why is this happening to me again?

I try to walk as far away from them as possible. I practically rub my shoulder against the opposite wall full of lockers to stay clear. I avoid all eye contact. I stare at my feet and put one foot in front of the other. Maybe they won't even know I'm there. But as I get closer I can hear them. Maggie says something about her project, though I can't quite hear what. Just as I'm about to pass them, my shirt snags on a locker, holding me in place. I tug myself clear, but it tears a hole in the sleeve and scratches my arm underneath. Ouch.

"Look, Maggie," Mr. Hart says. "The rest of the class managed to turn in their models on time. I already gave you an extension over spring break. So you turn it in today or you get an F."

"I told you what happened," Maggie said. "It wasn't my fault." She sounds desperate.

I should just keep going.

Or maybe I could fix this after all. I take a deep breath and walk closer. "It's true," I say.

Mr. Hart and Maggie stare at me. Maggie's eyes grow big and a little wild. She slowly shakes her head back and forth as if that could make me disappear.

I smile, acting friendly like Josh suggested, so Maggie can see I'm trying to help her. They don't say anything, so I start again. "Mr. Hart, really, it's true. I saw her project on the bus this morning. It looked great. But then I bumped into her, and her project got kind of crushed. It was my fault. I'm really sorry."

There, that should fix it. I hold my hand over my torn shirt and try to smile even though my arm hurts.

Mr. Hart lifts the towel, uncovering Maggie's model. The inside of the box is smeared with black paint. It's a mess of colored spheres, tape, and tangled fishing line.

"I'm disappointed in you, Maggie. First you tell me you need more time. Then you tell me that a dachshund boarding at your grandmother's clinic chewed up your solar system model . . ."

Oh no. Maggie must have come up with some other excuse, and now I blew it.

Mr. Hart looks back and forth between us. "And now," he says, "you're getting your new friend to cover for you? You really need to take responsibility for your own work, Maggie MacKenzie."

My smile is frozen on my face. Maggie is going to think I'm smiling because I'm happy she's in trouble. And Mr. Hart is going to think I'm dishonest and not let me adopt Chewie.

Josh never should have told me to "fix it by being friendly." Now look what's happened. I'm just not a smile-and-fix-it kind of girl.

"And what's this?" Mr. Hart asks, holding up a purple-painted Nerf ball.

"That one is, um, Pluto," Maggie says.

"You did not do your research, Maggie. Nor were you paying attention in class—or else you'd know that Pluto is no longer a planet."

Maggie's shoulders droop.

"So which is it, Maggie?" Mr. Hart says. "Did the dog eat your planets?" He looks at me. I have to get out of here before this gets any worse. "Or are you going to blame it on your new friend?"

"Both," Maggie says, looking right at me, "and she is *not* my friend!" She walks to the garbage can and dumps in what remains of her solar system model.

"I'm sorry," I say as I head to my class. "I'm really sorry."

"Get away from me," Maggie says. "And stay away!"

So I go. I go as fast as I can without actually running. I'm late to yet another class, and I definitely did not "fix it." My chance of ever becoming a Vet Volunteer is over. Especially if Maggie MacKenzie has any say.

Chapter Seven

. . . .

When we get home, Josh heads inside, and I check
the alley behind the store to see if the gray-and-
white-striped tabby cat is there. He's not.

I sit on the back step, waiting, then call, "Here,
Tabby, Tabby," but there is no trace of him.

I put fresh water from the outside spigot in the
water bowl. I hope that his torn ear is healing and
that he's all right. With the tabby nowhere in sight,
I head upstairs.

I drop my backpack on the couch next to Josh's.
Sophie is at the kitchen table, drawing. She shows
Josh and me her pictures full of butterflies, smiling
kids, and flowers. I wish I was still in elementary

school. Everything was a lot less complicated back then.

"How was school?" Mom asks.

"So far so good," says Josh.

"Me too," Sophie says. "We have a super tall slide on our playground. And I played with a girl named Jasmine."

I wonder if that's Sunita's little sister.

Josh pipes in with, "A kid named David Hutchinson showed me around school. He lives right down the street and he invited me over to his house over the weekend."

"He did?" I ask.

Josh nods.

How does he do it? How can Josh make friends on just his first day?

"How about you, Jules?" Mom asks.

I can't tell her all the awful stuff. "It was okay," I say. I'm not going to mention Maggie. "A girl named Sunita showed me around. Sophie, does Jasmine have a twin brother and a cat named Mittens?"

Sophie shrugs. "I don't know. Why?"

"Because Sunita has a little sister named Jasmine."

I look at Josh to see if he's going to help me out and bring up the subject of Chewie. He's not. In fact, he looks like he's enjoying watching me struggle for words. I take a deep breath and continue. "I have a really cool science teacher, Mr. Hart. He has lots of animals in his classroom." I wait for Mom to look up so I can see how she's feeling—so I can see if I should tell her more.

"That's great," Mom says, busy with the salad she's making. Now's not a good time to ask her about Chewie. How am I going to get her permission?

"I knew you would both do just fine," Mom says, this time looking up. "Do you have any homework?"

"Not much," Josh says.

"Yeah, me neither," I say.

"Good," says Mom. "Your dad would like you both to meet some of our neighbors with him before dinner, to say hi and introduce the store. It'll be good for business."

"Okay," Josh says. "I'll tell him we're home."

I'd rather not go meet a bunch of strangers after the bad day I've had. But since Mom and Dad both lost their jobs in Pittsburgh, I've wanted to help out however I can. We have to make the store work. Plus, if I say no, it'll make Dad unhappy. If I volunteer to help, maybe it'll put him in a good mood so I can talk to him about adopting

Chewie. "I'll go, too," I say, and run after Josh.

"What about me?" Sophie says.

But Mom tells her, "Next time."

I catch up with Josh before he enters the store. "Don't forget," I say. "You have to help me convince Mom and Dad about Chewie. They have to send a signed permission note."

"You need help—that's for sure!" Josh says. "Step one: Did you think of a better name than Chewie?"

"No," I say. "Not yet."

Dad's on the phone when we enter the store. He smiles, waves, and holds up one finger, motioning that he'll be just a minute.

While Dad's on the phone, Josh and I sit on one of the empty displays and whisper ideas for less-destructive-sounding bunny names. "How about Leo?" Josh says.

"It's a girl," I say.

"Um, Jules, I think a girl rabbit is a bad idea. What if she gets outside? Won't we end up with a bunch of little baby rabbits hopping all over the place?"

"I'd make sure she stays safe inside the house. And anyway, I have a coupon to get her spayed."

"At Dr. Mac's?" Josh asks.

"Yes, but I was thinking maybe I could take her to the shelter instead of to Dr. Mac."

"I thought you were going to fix that whole Maggie situation?"

"I tried," I whisper. "It didn't work out."

By the time Dad gets off the phone, our final name choices are on a list tucked into my pocket for safekeeping: Cinnamon, Cuddles, Mrs. Dandelion, Auntie Whiskers, and Hip-Hop. Josh thinks Cuddles is our best chance. I prefer Auntie Whiskers or Mrs. Dandelion. Still, Cuddles sounds the tamest. Who wouldn't fall in love with a sweet bunny named Cuddles?

"Okay," Dad says, finally hanging up the phone. "Time to be neighborly. I've got a list of the local merchants I'd like to give flyers to today about our grand opening. We'll start together so you'll get the idea, then I think we'll need to divvy up the list in order to reach everyone. I promised your mother we'd be back in time for dinner. Are you ready to meet and greet?"

Josh and I nod. Dad hands us each a folder full of flyers and grabs a canvas bag full of yardsticks with "WRENCHES & ROSES" and the store phone number and address printed on them.

Ready or not, here we go.

The copy shop is the first place we stop. Dad's a

pro. He made the flyers there, so he already knows the owners.

"Hello," he says. "I'm back. I want you to meet my kids." He introduces us, tells them about the grand-opening sale, and asks if he can leave a few flyers and some 15-percent-off coupons on their bulletin board.

For forty-five minutes, the three of us drop in together at the craft store, a women's clothing store, and a Laundromat. Dad introduces us again and again, and asks each neighbor if they need him to carry any particular items in our new store.

"We're here to help," Dad says. "Just let me know what you need." He gives everyone his business card, a flyer, and a free yardstick. Dad is super good at being friendly. Josh smiles, answers questions, and tells everybody how much he likes Ambler. I just stand there, listening and nodding, and trying to smile without looking too fake.

"Great job, you two," Dad says as we leave the deli.

"I think you get the idea," he says. "Just be friendly, introduce yourself, and tell them briefly about Wrenches and Roses. Give them a free yardstick no matter what. Got it?"

Josh and I nod.

"Okay," Dad says. "Josh, see if you can hit these three shops on the other side of the street. Jules, how about you drop in on the bakery and the yoga studio—"

"Wait," I say, "aren't Josh and I going together?"

"No," Dad says, smiling and handing me a couple of yardsticks. "Not enough time. Divide and conquer—you can do it, Jules. Let's all meet in front of the sporting goods store one block down—in fifteen minutes, okay?"

"Okay," Josh says, heading across the street with his list and yardsticks.

"Okay," I say. I pause and take a deep breath. I do not want to disappoint Dad. This is a family business and I can do this.

I'm still telling myself, *I can do this, I can do this* as I push open the door of the yoga studio.

New age music is playing quietly in the background, and the door squeaks closed behind me. There's a yoga class going on beyond the curtain in the next room. I don't want to interrupt the class, but a slim woman in a purple tank top and black yoga pants gets up from her mat in the back of the room and asks if she can help me.

"Are you interested in joining our class?" she whispers.

"Oh no. I'm so sorry to interrupt. I just wanted to introduce myself."

The woman smiles and raises her eyebrows. *I can do this, I can do this.*

I smile back at her. "I'm Jules and my mom and dad bought the hardware store. It's a family business—Wrenches and Roses. We have garden stuff, too." I'm not sure what to say next, so I reach for the flyers. "We're having an opening sale. Here's a flyer and a discount coupon if there is anything you or your yoga studio needs."

"Thanks," she says, tucking the flyer and coupon under the counter.

"Oh, I almost forgot," I say, juggling the remaining flyers and coupons. "Here's a free . . ." Oh no, I drop the two yardsticks and they go clattering to the floor. "Sorry, sorry. A free yardstick," I say, picking them up and giving her one.

"Thank you. And bye now," she says in a quiet but firm voice.

I tiptoe toward the door, gripping the last yardstick so I don't drop it. I try to open the door quietly, but it has a loud squeak. I think about telling her that our store carries a great spray that stops squeaks, but I leave before I make any more noise.

Three buildings down, the bakery is full of customers and lots of noise, thank goodness. It smells great, too. I wish I'd brought some money. I'd buy a fresh baguette for dinner to surprise Mom. I stand there, breathing in the great aroma of freshly baked bread. That and the warmth relaxes me.

I can do this, I tell myself again when a man behind the counter asks what I need. I introduce myself and tell him about Wrenches & Roses and give him the flyer, coupon, and yardstick.

"Thank you, my dear," he says. "I'm glad someone is opening the hardware store again. Bread stick?" He offers me one covered in sesame seeds.

"Oh, no thank you," I say.

He frowns. "No one turns down Mario's bread sticks. It hurts my feelings."

"It looks great, and smells even better," I say. "I just didn't bring any money."

"For you, Jules, a free bread stick," he says with a big smile. He hands it to me over the counter. "You gave me a lovely measuring stick, after all. Besides, I insist."

"Okay, thanks!" I say.

"Take a bite. How is it?"

"Perfect," I say, chewing. Now I'm smiling, too. I guess I can meet people after all. "You know," I say between bites, pointing at the torn window screen behind Mario and the upper window, which is propped open with a wooden spoon, "Wrenches and Roses sells screening, and my dad knows how to repair everything. He sells all the hardware and can tell you how to fix stuff."

"You are a good salesperson," Mario says. "Your family business will do well."

"I hope so," I say. "Thanks. And come by the store anytime."

"I will," Mario says. "I will."

Wow, that went so much better than the yoga studio. I can't wait to tell Dad and Josh.

When I get to the sporting goods store one block down, Dad is waiting outside, and Josh is just coming out of the door.

"How'd it go?" Dad asks me.

"The yoga studio—so-so, but the bakery was great. Mario, the owner, was super nice."

Dad puts a hand on my shoulder. "You're both really helping," he says. "Now just one more stop on my list. It's on the way home. We can all go together. I saved the best for last—the veterinary clinic."

The veterinary clinic? Ugh, that's got to be Maggie MacKenzie's grandmother's clinic. And Sunita told me Maggie lives there. Dad is in a great mood now and I want to keep helping, but I can't risk ruining everything with another run-in with Maggie.

Chapter Eight

. . . .

I'll skip the vet's," I say. "I need to head home and get started on my homework."

"Oh, come on, Jules," Dad says. "I know how much you love animals—maybe there will be some you can pet." He's heading up the walkway to the clinic.

A sign out front says

DR. MAC'S PLACE
DR. J. J. MACKENZIE

Three run-ins with Maggie are enough for one day. I can't handle another. Plus, I doubt having the veterinarian's granddaughter hate me is good for Mom and Dad's business. They'll probably find out sooner or later, but I'd rather avoid their disappointment today.

"We'll only be a few minutes," Dad says. "Then it's home for dinner."

I make eye contact with Josh so he'll help me out of this, but all he says is "Yeah, Jules, let's check it out. Maybe we'll see some cats and dogs or maybe even something exotic—a snake or a ferret or something."

I have no choice but to follow them in.

A bell jangles as we enter the clinic, but no one is there except a huge orange tabby half asleep on the counter. He looks up at us, blinks his eyes as if he is bored with our company, then curls back up again.

"Hello," Dad calls out.

A big old basset hound galumphs in from a side room to greet us. I stay behind Josh, near the front exit, eyeing the door the basset hound came from. Maggie could be right behind him.

"Hello, buddy," Josh says, bending to pet the dog.

Still, no one comes out. "Well, let's just sit and wait a few moments," Dad says, sitting in one of the waiting room chairs.

"No, we'd better go," I say. "They're probably already closed."

"It's only five forty-five," Dad says. "The sign says they are open until six, the door was unlocked, and the lights are all on."

The basset comes to sniff my ankles, wagging his tail. He leans against my legs and looks up at me with his big, sad eyes. He's kind of drooly, but cute. I can't help myself—I have to give him some pats. Then some rubs around his ears. He loves it and lies on his side, so I give him a good belly rub.

Down the hall, a door labeled Dolittle Room opens, and David Hutchinson, the kid who showed Josh around school, pokes his head out. He's cradling something tiny wrapped in a towel against his chest. A tiny squeak comes from the bundle.

"Oh hi," David says, smiling when he sees Josh. "Dr. Mac is a little busy right now. Is there an emergency?"

"No, no, not at all," Dad says, standing up. "Take your time. We just wanted to stop in and say hello. We can come back tomorrow."

"I'll tell Dr. Mac you're here," David says. He disappears back into the exam room, but he keeps the door open. The basset hound rolls over to his feet and makes his rounds to Dad. The dog wags his tail and looks up expectantly until Dad gives him some pats and ruffles his long ears.

I hear more tiny squeaks from the room. I want

to look in, but I don't want to see Maggie or have her see me. Josh walks slowly toward the open door. I nudge him forward and whisper, "Give me a signal if Maggie's in there."

As Josh gets closer to the door, a tall woman with short white hair, glasses, and blue eyes comes out to the hallway. She's holding a tiny gray kitten with its eyes still closed, wrapped in a towel, too. "I'm Dr. Mac," she says.

Dad introduces all three of us.

"David tells me you bought the hardware store?" Dr. Mac says. "And I see Sherlock Holmes is saying hello," she adds, nodding toward the old basset hound, who is licking my hands and won't leave my side. He's so affectionate.

"My daughter has a way with animals," Dad says.

"A sixth sense," Josh pipes in.

"I can see that," says Dr. Mac. "I'll be with you in just a minute."

Behind her I can hear faint but persistent squeaky little mews. The kittens must be very young. Josh peeks in.

"You can take a look if you want," Dr. Mac says.

Josh goes in. Dad and I are right behind him.

Luckily, Maggie is not there, just David, Dr. Mac, and five of the tiniest, cutest kittens I've ever seen.

Two are gray, two are black, and there's a little calico, too. I smell the familiar kitty smell, just like at the shelter in Pittsburgh. Man, do I miss volunteering there.

David is sitting in a chair with a towel on his lap, holding a black kitten and feeding it from a tiny bottle. Dr. Mac unwraps and weighs the one she was holding. Three more kittens are all on top of each other in a blanket-lined cardboard box, little squeaky mews calling, their tiny paws moving as they inch about on their bellies.

None of them have open eyes. They are so adorable.

"Someone left them on the clinic doorstep this morning, with a note that they were found in the high school parking lot," Dr. Mac says. "We don't know what happened to their mother, but they're only a day or two old."

"How can you tell?" Josh asks.

"Their umbilical cord stubs are still attached, and they only weigh about four ounces each."

Dr. Mac puts the kitten she just weighed back in the box with its siblings and picks up another one. She tests the temperature of the small bottle of kitty formula on her wrist and feeds the new kitten, who paws at the bottle with skinny legs and the tiniest pink-padded paws. When the kitten sucks the bottle, his ears wiggle back and forth in concentration. His little face is too cute, eyes closed, with drops of formula on his fuzzy muzzle.

"They're so tiny. Are they going to be okay without their mother?" I ask.

"Well, they'd be much better off being cared for by her. A mama cat's milk has colostrum, which helps prevent infection and disease. Without their mother's milk, they are more susceptible to all kinds of illnesses. So we have to keep them warm and hydrated and growing with this kitty formula. We'll need to feed them every one to two hours and weigh them every day to make sure they are gaining weight. And of course watch them carefully for any signs of dehydration, illness, or parasites. They were covered with fleas when we got them, so we've used a special kitten-safe flea formula and combed out all the fleas. Kittens can become anemic from fleas."

David holds his little black kitten upright against his chest and pats its back. "Burping it, like a baby," he says with a smile. "Too bad they don't make kitty diapers."

I never worked with kittens this young in Pittsburgh. Those kittens always had their eyes open and could walk around a little.

Josh steps forward and asks exactly what I'm thinking. "Do you need any help feeding the others?"

I'm ready to wash my hands and get right to work, but Dr. Mac says, "No thanks, David has helped me feed all five this time. And my granddaughter, Maggie, will be home from basketball practice any minute now. She'll help with the next feedings. By tomorrow, I'm hoping the Feral Cat Rescue Society can find a suitable foster family or two to take care of them until they are old enough to be adopted out. It's a lot of work, feeding them and keeping them clean twenty-four hours a day."

I look at Dad, hoping he'll volunteer our family, but he doesn't. He just says how cute the kittens are and gives his little talk about the hardware store and says he's sorry to bother Dr. Mac when she's so busy.

"Oh, no bother," Dr. Mac says. "Nice to meet you all. Looks like you know David already, so you'll have to meet Maggie next time around."

Josh smiles and says, "I think my sister and I have already met Maggie, right, Jules?"

I nod and, cute kittens or not, suddenly have the urge to get out of there as fast as I can.

Chapter Nine

. . . .

When we get home, I can't help thinking how cool it'd be to volunteer at Dr. Mac's. But I shake the thought from my head because after all my arguments with Maggie, I'm sure it's impossible. I'll volunteer at the local shelter instead. Of course now Josh and I have to focus on our Chewie plan. We've got just a few minutes before dinner, so we have to figure out our best strategy. Sophie won't leave Josh's room, so we have to let her in on the plan, too.

"I can keep a secret!" Sophie promises.

"You'd better! Now, Jules, step one," Josh says. "Your adorable rabbit is now named Cuddles."

"Sounds good. Cuddles it is," I reply.

"Step two," Josh says. "We write a permission note all ready and easy for signing, except we avoid using Cuddles's old name or her new name. Okay?"

"Okay," I say.

Josh types the permission note on his computer and prints it out.

Dear Mr. Hart,
Our daughter, Julia Darrow, has permission to adopt the science classroom rabbit. We understand that owning a pet is a big respon-sibility, and will supervise Julia as she takes care of the rabbit.
    Thank you for providing the cage, litter box, and water bottle.
Sincerely,
John and Lynn Darrow

"Do you really think we can get Mom and Dad to sign it?" I ask.

"That's step three," Josh says. "Just leave it to me, but have the note and a pen nearby during dinner. We'll wait for a good moment, and then I'll bring it up. Agreed?"

"Agreed," I say. "And Sophie, don't say anything, okay?"

"Okay," Sophie says. Sophie loves being in on a secret, but she usually blows it. I hope she can keep quiet tonight.

• • • • •

During dinner Mom and Dad talk about the details of opening the hardware store.

"We can't have any spots on the miniature roses at the cash register," Mom says.

"I know, no spots," Dad says.

"After all, the store is called Wrenches and Roses, so the roses have to be perfect."

"Right," Dad says. Even Dad is looking tired and stressed. He's got bags under his eyes. He needs more sleep.

I keep looking at Josh, but he shakes his head, telling me the time is not right to bring up Chewie—I mean Cuddles.

"Good pasta, Mom," Josh finally says. "May I have more, please?"

"Of course," Mom says. "Help yourself."

We're getting nowhere, and dinner is almost over.

"Want to hear about my new school?" Sophie asks.

I shake my head, but Josh says, "Sure."

"We have a pet rat named Ratty," Sophie says.

"Huh," Mom says. "That's an interesting animal for a classroom. Some people think rats are pests, not pets. By the way"—she turns to my dad—"did you order rat traps to carry in the store?"

Dad nods, and Sophie frowns. She looks like she is about to cry. Poor Sophie. I want to take her mind off what I'm sure she is picturing—her classroom pet stuck in a trap. Ugh. So I try to think how to bring up the topic of another class-room pet—Chewie.

I lean toward Sophie, and the pen in my pocket pokes me in the leg. "My science teacher wants me to adopt the classroom rabbit," I blurt out. Josh looks at me like I'm crazy.

What was I thinking? I should have left this to Josh, but I keep going. "He said the rabbit needs a new home, so I should give it a try. We'd be doing Mr. Hart a favor."

Josh and Sophie stare at me wide-eyed. Mom and Dad stop eating and stare at me, too.

"He said he would give us the cage and water bottle and litter box, too," I say, "so that won't cost us a thing. I can buy rabbit food with my allow-ance, and we already have fresh produce like bits of lettuce and carrot nubs we'd be throwing out anyway."

Mom and Dad look at each other.

"Did you already tell your teacher yes?" Mom asks.

"I told him I would ask," I say. That's mostly true.

"You promised we could get a pet," Sophie says. "Please! Pretty please with hopping bunnies on top!"

"A rabbit would be a whole lot better than a rat," Josh says.

Dad laughs and looks at Mom. "I think we're outnumbered."

Mom does not seem convinced. She sighs. "How big is this rabbit, and where would we put him?"

"Her," I say. "She's really small, a dwarf with lop ears. She's used to being indoors in her cage. So Sophie and I can keep her in our room. Later, maybe I can build her an agility corral in the basement, once we clean it up. You're going to love her, Mom. She's got the softest brown and white fur. Plus, she's litter-box trained. And when Dad and I build some planter boxes filled with roses for the front of the store, the rabbit droppings will make good compost. We could even sell the compost in the store." I try not to twist the permission note under the table.

"Caring for a pet is a big responsibility," Mom says.

"I know. I'll take care of her, Mom, I promise. You won't have to do a thing."

"I'll help," Josh says.

"Me too," says Sophie.

"She's totally adorable," I say. "I just know she'll be a really great family pet!"

"What is this adorable rabbit's name?" Mom asks.

"Cuddles," Josh, Sophie, and I say in unison.

Dad winks at me.

Mom looks at Dad. "We did promise a pet," Mom says. "But I think we should try it on a one-week trial basis. If you take good care of her, do all your other chores, and keep up with your school-work, you can keep her."

I pull the folded permission note and pen from under the table.

"What's this?" Mom says.

"A permission letter. You have to sign it, and we have to pick up Ch— er, Cuddles—tomorrow after school."

Mom and Dad both read the letter.

Josh is smiling. Sophie claps and says, "Yippee, we're getting a bunny."

"Wait a sec," Mom says, taking the note and pen. "Before we all start celebrating . . ."

She signs the note then adds:

P.S. We'd like to have Cuddles join
us for a one-week trial basis. If that
is agreeable to you, we will pick up
Cuddles, her cage, and supplies on
Tuesday afternoon.
Thank you.

Mom adds our phone number to the note and hands it back to me.

My heart flip-flops as I read it. What if Mr. Hart doesn't like our giving Chewie a new name? What if he decides just to send her to a foster home instead? Josh stands up and gives Mom and Dad a hug. So do Sophie and I.

"Nothing's going to go wrong," Josh says. "You won't regret it."

Sophie hops around the kitchen, singing, "Yay, yay, yay!"

Mom sighs again. "I think I regret it already," she says, but she says it with a big smile. I feel like singing yay, too, but instead I take the note and say, "Thanks, Mom and Dad. You're going to love Cuddles."

But I think, *One week. I have to keep everything perfect for just one week.*

Chapter Ten

. . . .

I avoid Maggie on the bus ride to school and watch out for her in the halls. She must be watching out for me, too, because I don't see her. The best part of the morning is when I see Chewie in science class. I rush to class early and give the note to Mr. Hart.

"Cuddles?" he says, raising his eyebrows as he reads the permission note with Mom's one-week trial-period proclamation. I hold my breath, hoping he won't change his mind. He walks over to Chewie's cage. "You hear that, Cuddles?" he asks. "You'd better behave for a week, at least."

Chewie sits on her hind paws, puts her front paws on the cage, and sniffs Mr. Hart's fingers. Her little nose and whiskers wiggle. She is so cute. Mr. Hart turns to me. "Your mom is coming today, right?"

"Yes," I say.

"I'll have two of my eighth-period students take Cuddles here down to the office after school."

"Thank you!" I say. I open the top of the cage and pet Chewie. It's hard to think of her as Cuddles.

"Now, be sure to make an appointment with Dr. MacKenzie," Mr. Hart says. "Cuddles is six months old already, so it's time to have her spayed."

"Okay, I'll make an appointment," I say. But I don't say I'll make it with Dr. MacKenzie.

The morning goes by quickly, and at lunch I tell Sunita that Mom is picking Josh and me up after school. "And Chewie, too," I say.

"That's great," Sunita says. "I've got to be quick at lunch today. Hope you don't mind finishing up alone. I promised Brenna, another Vet Volunteer, that I'd help her get ready for her Save Our Streams meeting on Thursday."

"Sure, that's fine," I say.

"And remember to come to the library at lunchtime on Thursday. Brenna is going to be speaking at both lunch periods about Stream Cleanup Day. Everyone is helping out."

"Okay," I say. "Sounds fun."

"Great," Sunita says, packing up her lunch. "I'll see you in gym later today. Don't forget we're on Tuesday-Thursday block scheduling this afternoon."

"Right," I say. "See you later."

It's hard sitting there alone for the rest of lunch, and even worse when I remember that Maggie has the same block gym schedule as Sunita and me. The overcooked cafeteria spaghetti suddenly feels like a big lump in my belly. I see Josh back at his locker right after my math class.

"I'm worried, Josh. I'm going to be in the same gym class as Maggie," I tell him. "What if it's dodgeball? You know how much I hate dodgeball. What if Maggie throws the ball at me?"

Josh grabs his books. "I'm sure it won't be dodgeball, and even if it is, Maggie can't be that bad," he says.

"You have no idea what it's like when someone hates you," I say. "You should have seen the way she looked at me in the hall yesterday. Can you walk to the office with me and help me convince them I need to transfer into a different gym class?"

"No," Josh says. "Just deal with it, Jules. Stay on the other side of the gym. Give Maggie plenty of space until things cool down. But eventually you might try talking to her and, you know, being friendly."

"Some help you are."

"Look," Josh says, "after seeing David and those kittens at Dr. Mac's yesterday, I want to hang out with the Vet Volunteers. The office is right down the street, and David and Sunita are really nice. Plus, Dr. Mac seems great, too. So if you want to keep avoiding Maggie, fine. But I'm not going to let you stop me from making friends or doing cool stuff."

"But, Josh—"

He slams his locker shut. "It's your problem, Jules, not mine," he says. "I have to get to class. I'll see you at the end of the day to get Chewie."

"Cuddles," I say.

"Right, Cuddles." Josh walks away, down the hall.

Josh usually knows how to make me feel better, but today he makes me feel worse.

Luckily, as soon as Josh leaves, I see Sunita walking toward me. I'm happy to see her. I know it hasn't even been two days, but I feel like Sunita and I could be friends.

"Hi, Jules!" she calls out as she waves to me. "Come on, I'll show you the best way to get to the gym."

Ugh. It's not just Maggie I'm worried about. I hate gym. It's the only subject in school I don't do well in. I'm not athletic at all, and I'd much rather be reading a book than running around the track out of breath. But off we go to the gymnasium, where Sunita shows me to the locker room so we can put away our book bags and get changed.

"What do you think we'll be doing in class today?" I ask Sunita.

I guess I must sound anxious because she smiles and says, "Don't worry, I'm not great in gym, either. It's not too bad here. Before spring break, we were doing a unit on basketball skills. Dribbling, shooting, layups. It wasn't too hard."

Basketball. Great. The perfect sport for a short, uncoordinated seventh-grader. We walk into the gym, and Sunita introduces me to the teacher, Ms. Donnelly, who puts me into a line based on my last name. As she takes attendance, I look around. The gym is huge, with hardwood floors and championship banners in the rafters. There are volleyball nets tucked into a corner and racks of basketballs toward the front.

And then there's Maggie. She's sitting two rows away from me, twirling a basketball on her finger and chatting with a male teacher. He's wearing a jacket that says COACH WILLIAMS on the back.

"Okay, kids!" Ms. Donnelly yells. "I hope you

all got a chance to practice your layups over the break. We've already reviewed the rules of basketball, so we're going to get to the exciting part: playing the game. Coach Williams from the girls' basketball team is here to observe and give tips."

Coach Williams waves. He looks friendly enough.

Ms. Donnelly points to Maggie and another girl. "Maggie and Darla, as two of Ambler's basketball stars, I'd like you each to be captains and choose teams. Then we'll play five on five and switch players from the bleachers every ten minutes. All right, let's get started!"

Maggie and Darla step onto the court. I'm sure I'll be chosen last. I always am. That's okay with me—I prefer to be as invisible as possible in gym class. With any luck, I can make it through the whole class without having to play. But what if Darla chooses me and I have to play against Maggie? I slump as low as possible and wish Sunita and I had sat farther back in the bleachers.

Darla and Maggie start calling out names. To my surprise, after six girls are called, Maggie turns to me, smiles, and says, "Jules."

I get up slowly and walk down to stand with her team. This is so confusing. Why'd she pick me? Before I even have time to wonder, Maggie and

Darla are finishing choosing their teams, and I'm on the court with nine other girls.

Okay, I think. *What would Josh do?* Deal with it. Be friendly. How awful could it be? Josh said Maggie can't be all that bad. She chose me, after all. Maybe Maggie's trying to be friendly, too? At least it's not dodgeball, right? We've probably used up three minutes already. So just seven minutes left?

I look up to the bleachers, and Sunita gives me a thumbs-up. Sunita said yesterday that Maggie is great at sports, so if the ball comes to me, I'll just pass it to Maggie. That's friendly, right? I can do this.

Coach Williams blows his whistle, and Maggie starts out with the ball. I hang back, away from the basket, not really sure what to do. Luckily, Sunita was right. Maggie is awesome at basketball. A tough-looking girl on the other team tries to steal the ball from her, but Maggie fakes a pass, moves quickly to her right, and in a split second she is under the basket, laying it in. Score!

The other girls on our team cheer and high-five Maggie. I can't help but feel a little excited, too. I clap twice, and then look to where I should go next. Now we are on defense, which is usually what I like, because it means I can make a show of playing without actually doing much. But it doesn't look like that's going to work on Maggie's team.

"Jules, guard Sarah! Right next to you!" Maggie yells to me.

I look to my right and see the tough girl with the ball. She's taller and stronger than me, and I really don't know how to guard someone, anyway. But maybe this is my chance to make things up to Maggie. My heart races and I run toward Sarah, trying to get between her and the basket. But she's way faster than I am, and she's already raising the basketball, ready to shoot. I lunge with my hand out, trying to block it. The only thing that gets blocked is my nose, with Sarah's elbow.

"Ow!" I yell as I hit the ground with a clumsy thud. My nose burns with pain, and my eyes smart with tears.

Maggie runs over to me. "Are you okay?" she pants.

I reach for my nose and touch it carefully. It's not bleeding and I don't think it's broken, but it hurts like crazy and the whole gym class saw me get knocked down. How embarrassing is that? I'm a terrible athlete, and now I'm lying on the floor with everyone looking down at me. Maggie made me look so stupid—all because she told me to guard Sarah.

"Why did you tell me to go after Sarah?" I ask, trying to stand. "You knew there was no way I could stop her from making a basket. I'm sorry I ruined your project and said that thing about the tutor, but you didn't have to do this to me!"

"Do what? What are you talking about?" Maggie shakes her head. "It's just a basketball game. I had no idea you were going to get hurt."

Coach Williams runs over. "Okay, ladies, break it up. Jules, are you okay?" He leans over and looks at my nose. "It seems fine, but take a break for the rest of class. You can go get changed."

I head back to the locker room, my eyes burning, my nose throbbing. I can't look at Maggie, Sunita, or anyone else. I just want this day to be over.

• • • • •

At the end of the day, Mom is parked in front of the school, just as planned. At least that's one good thing. Josh and I carry Chewie in her cage across the lawn to the car and put her on the backseat. Mom and Sophie help carry the extra food and a backup water bottle.

"So this is Cuddles?" Mom asks.

I try to calm the rabbit down. She's hopping back and forth in the cage one minute, then cowering in the corner the next. I don't think she likes all the jostling around.

"Isn't she cute?" I say.

Mom and Sophie nod.

I can't wait to get Chewie—I mean Cuddles—home. I have to start thinking of her and calling her Cuddles.

Cuddles, Cuddles, Cuddles. Her name is Cuddles.

But the minute we get home, Cuddles is anything but cuddly. Sophie wants me to take her out of the cage so she can hold her.

"Okay," I say, "but just for a few minutes. Rabbits do not like to be held that much."

I make Sophie sit on the floor and put a pillow on her lap. Josh closes the door to the bedroom, then holds the cage door open while I lift Cuddles out. I try to hold her close to my body, but Cuddles thumps her back feet. She nearly leaps out of my arms, and her nails scratch me. But I hold her and get her safely to Sophie's lap. Cuddles seems nervous. Maybe the car ride agitated her.

Josh and I sit on the floor on both sides of Sophie and Cuddles. We pet the rabbit until she calms down a little. But she is curious, her nose and whiskers twitching. She wants to explore. She sniffs and hops, sniffs and stops, tentatively at first, then she's hopping all over. She goes under

Sophie's bed with Sophie giggling like crazy.

"Look, look." Sophie is over-the-top excited, her voice screechy and fast. She's practically hopping as much as Cuddles. "She's under the bed. There she is!" Sophie shouts. "She's hopping again!" Sophie bounces on the mattress on her knees, then leans over upside down to watch Cuddles.

Cuddles hops out again and begins to chew on the cord to my desk lamp.

"No, no, Cuddles," I say. I quickly unplug the lamp and move the cord up where she can't reach it. Then she starts pulling the books off our lower shelf with her front paws and chewing on them.

"My book!" Sophie howls. "She's ruining my favorite book!"

I grab the book and shoo Cuddles away from the shelf.

"I see why your teacher named her Chewie," Josh says.

"Okay, Cuddles goes back in her cage until we can bunny proof our room," I say. I put her back in her cage and latch the lid. Cuddles immediately puts her front paws on the cage and sits up on her hind feet, sniffing at the air as if she wants out again.

"Look, look!" Sophie laughs. "Cuddles pooped under my bed. I'm not cleaning that up. You have to, Jules!"

"Fine," I say. "Josh, could you please bring me a paper towel? But don't tell Mom why, okay?"

"Sure," Josh says. He leaves the room, closing the door behind him again.

Sophie jumps around the room, chanting, "We have a bunny, we have a bunny!" Cuddles starts to chew on the wire of her cage. Then she chews on the plastic edge of her water bottle, instead of drinking from the little metal pipe.

"Sophie, quit jumping around. You're making her nervous," I say.

Sophie finally calms down but wants to be right next to the cage. She sits on the carpet in front of Cuddles. Sophie pulls out her homework and a book she brought home from school. Just then, Cuddles chews a big hole through the bottom edge of her water bottle. Water gushes out in spurts right on Sophie's book, her homework, the carpet, and of course on Sophie.

Sophie jumps up screaming, "Look what she did!"

"Shh!" I say, moving Sophie away from Cuddles and the wet mess.

Josh comes back in. "What's going on?" he asks.

"We're going to need more paper towels," I whisper.

Chapter Eleven

• • • • • • • • • • • •

Wednesday morning before school, I clean out Cuddles's cage and give her fresh food and fresh water in the water bottle I replaced the night before, then Sophie, Josh, and I all take turns petting her. She is so sweet and funny. But I need a backup water bottle or two for now if her chewing continues. I get to science class early so I can ask Mr. Hart where I can buy more.

"Did she chew through another one already?" he asks.

"Yes," I say. "Does she do that often?"

Mr. Hart nods. "Give her plenty of chew toys. And get her spayed soon."

"Right," I say, "but there's no rush, is there?

Getting her spayed, I mean. If I don't have any male rabbits around her, she can't get pregnant, right?"

"Getting her spayed isn't just for preventing overpopulation of rabbits. Getting her spayed will keep her calmer. She'll live a longer, happier, healthier life, too. You still have the coupon for Dr. Mac's, right?"

"Yes." I say. But I'm careful not to promise to use it. Instead, I'm wondering how many weeks' allowance it will cost me to have her spayed somewhere else. I'd rather not run into Maggie.

After school, Josh goes to Wrenches & Roses to help Dad, and Sophie and I take Cuddles out of her cage to let her hop around the room.

We pet her and feed her some carrots and try to keep her from chewing all the wrong things— the bedposts, more books, the comforter hanging from the bed, Sophie's doll. You name it, Cuddles wants to chew it. I put her back in her cage, then check her new water bottle. Sure enough, she's chewed a small hole in the new one, too. Water is dribbling out, soaking the clean newspapers I just added to the bottom of her cage.

"Sophie, can you please go ask Mom if she has any extra newspaper?" I ask.

"Okay," Sophie says. She runs out of the room.

That's two bottles she's ruined in less than twenty-four hours. I'll need to buy a glass water bottle at the pet store. She won't be able to chew through that. I hope they're not too expensive.

"Cuddles," I tell her, "you'd better behave. We're not rich, you know."

Cuddles tilts her head and twitches her nose, looking cuter than ever.

"Fine, you're worth it," I say. "But no more chewing stuff you're not supposed to, okay?"

The shelter is not too far past the pet store. I'll drop in there today, too, and show them my recommendation letter and ask about volunteering. And I'll make an appointment for getting Cuddles spayed at the shelter so I can avoid Maggie and her grandmother's clinic. Sure, it'd be free at Dr. Mac's and more convenient. And of course it'd be great to be a Vet Volunteer with Sunita and David and Josh, but I don't think that'd ever be possible after I've messed up so much with Maggie. Besides, I don't need to be a Vet Volunteer to be around lots of animals. I have Cuddles. There are tons of animals in Mr. Hart's science class, and I can volunteer at the shelter. It's kind of a long walk to get there, but exercise is good for people and pets.

I go sit in the back alley, planning my walk and

reading over the bunny facts again to see if there is anything else I need to buy at the pet store. I watch and wait, too, to see if the gray tabby is around.

Sophie sits down next to me with a pile of newspapers.

"If you sit quietly," I say, "we can see if the tabby cat will come for a visit."

After a few moments Sophie is fidgety and bored, so I read her the bunny facts pamphlet. That quiets her down.

"Remember, most rabbits do not like to be picked up or held in your lap," I say.

"Why not?" Sophie asks.

"They just don't," I say. "And that's what the pamphlet says."

"Oh."

"Next, rabbits can be easily litter-box trained."

"Like Cuddles," Sophie says, "except when she poops under the bed."

"They are good at grooming themselves," I say, "but rabbits need to be brushed often and have their nails clipped periodically."

"I can brush her," Sophie says.

"Okay, great. Let's see, what else? Their teeth are always growing so they need hard things to chew."

I don't think Sophie will understand the next part so I don't read it out loud:

Neutering and spaying prevents or reduces undesirable behavior and increases female rabbits' life spans.

I look out over the back parking lot, thinking, *Okay, so maybe Cuddles needs to be spayed sooner rather than later to cut down on her chewing.* I'll make an appointment at the shelter right away.

"Is your tabby cat ever going to come back?" Sophie asks.

"I don't know," I say. I'm worried about him, but I don't want to worry Sophie. "He must have found his way home."

When I tell Mom I'm going for a walk to the pet store, she insists I take Sophie along and stop at the park for a while, too, so she can play.

Sophie is all smiles.

"All right," I say, "but you have to walk fast and keep up."

"I will."

When we start walking, I tell Sophie that after the pet store we're going someplace better than the park.

"Where?" she asks.

"To look at the cute dogs and cats at the shelter."

"Can we pet them?"

"I don't know. Sometimes you can pet them. Sometimes you're only allowed to look. We'll see when we get there."

It's a long walk to the shelter, but Sophie is a trouper, keeping up with my pace the whole way. The weather is warm, and I should have brought some human water bottles along for us. Luckily, there is a water fountain at the shelter.

Sophie and I look through the windows at the cats and dogs before I approach anyone at the counter. Even though we can't pet them unless we are with our parents, it relaxes me to be here and to see all the animals.

I work up my courage to approach the man behind the counter. I wonder what I should ask him about first. Volunteering or getting Cuddles spayed? I can't decide which, and then Sophie distracts me.

"Look, Jules," she says. "There's another room with rabbits and birds and a rat just like Ratty. Let's go look."

I peek through the window. Sophie is right. There are cages of rabbits, some birds, a snake, a lizard, a few hamsters, and a rat. I check the door, but it is locked. I wonder if all the rabbits waiting to be adopted chew on things, too. A teenager with a blue streak in her hair approaches and unlocks the door.

"Would you like to come in and see the small pets?" she asks.

"Yes," Sophie says, turning and giving me her biggest grin.

Sophie and I enter the room as the girl holds the door open for us. "Thanks," I say. As we pass, I read her name tag. It says LEAH, and underneath her name it says VOLUNTEER.

"So, what kind of small animal are you looking for?" Leah asks as she pulls out some portable fencing and begins to set it up.

"We already have a rabbit," Sophie says, peeking her nose close to every cage. "Her name is Cuddles."

"Cute name," says Leah. "Just one rabbit, though? Rabbits are very social creatures. They like companionship. I have three rabbits at home."

"What are their names?" Sophie asks.

"Marshmallow, Bert, and Cupcake. They love playing with each other," Leah says as she opens up the fencing to make a little corral on the floor about four feet wide. She adds a ball, some hard plastic baby toys, an open paper bag, a couple of cardboard boxes, and a cardboard tube.

"Are you going to play with the rabbits?" Sophie asks.

"Yes, they need more space than their cages for exercise, and they need to exercise every day. Plus, rabbits are very curious. They love to explore, burrow, shred stuff, and chew."

Leah opens one of the smaller cages and carries a bunny that she calls Lolli to the enclosure she made. Lolli makes a couple of excited leaps the moment she has room to play. She sniffs at one of the boxes, gnaws on the corner, then hops on top of it and looks around. Sophie laughs, but Lolli has just gotten started. When Leah adds another rabbit named Sunshine, the two sniff at each other, then chase the ball, each other, and hide out in the paper bag and cardboard tunnel.

"Our rabbit chews a lot of stuff," Sophie says. "Her name used to be Chewie."

Leah laughs. "That's a perfect name for a rabbit." She sits down inside the enclosure and closes it behind her. "Don't mind me," she says. "I'm just getting Lolli and Sunshine used to being friendly around people. It increases their chances of being adopted."

"You know a lot about rabbits," I say. "What do you do if your rabbits chew too much? Or if they chew stuff they're not supposed to?"

"Well, first off, give them plenty of nontoxic things to chew. Cardboard boxes like this one, an untreated wicker basket, carrots and veggies, of course, gobs of timothy hay, nontoxic wood or baby toys, willow balls, you name it. And believe me, if your bunny is bored, she'll find something to chew."

Sophie and I squat down to watch Lolli and Sunshine hop around.

"Jules," Sophie whispers too loudly in my ear. "Let's take Lolli home to play with instead of Cuddles." I shake my head and tell her to shush.

"My rabbit Bert loves to shred phone books," Leah says. "Give him a phone book and he's a happy camper, shredding it like it's his job. Rabbits are full of curiosity, so keep giving your rabbit new toys. I'm always making new agility activities like ramps and cardboard boxes or tubes full of paper for Bert and Cupcake to dig through. They love to chase each other and burrow and toss paper around. Cupcake likes to fetch things and rearrange and bunch up and push her own towel like a home decorator. And Marshmallow? He likes to sit and watch all the antics like a big, sweet lump. Each rabbit has its own personality and temperament. And if they have another rabbit or friendly pet to bond with, they'll have someone furry to snuggle and play with. Isn't that right, Lollipop?"

Lolli rubs her neck and chin against Leah's hand.

Sophie leans into my ear again. "We could bring Lolli home to play with Cuddles," she says. "Two rabbits are better, right?"

"Of course if you get two or more rabbits," Leah says, "be sure that they are all spayed or neutered before you put them together, or you'll have too many bunnies in no time. I've read that rabbits can reproduce about once every month with up to ten kits in each litter."

"We plan to get Cuddles spayed soon," I say. "Do you know how much it costs to do it here at the shelter?" I hold my breath, wondering if I can get Mom to pay me for babysitting Sophie. Or how many weeks of my saved allowances this will cost me.

"They only spay and neuter dogs and cats here. The best place to go for rabbits is Dr. MacKenzie on Main Street," Leah says.

"Are there any other vets in town?"

"Not that I know of," Leah says, petting Lolli and then Sunshine as she hops by. "Besides, not every vet knows how to care for rabbits. Dr. Mac is the greatest. You really should take your rabbit there."

This is not what I was hoping to hear. I start to

unzip my backpack pocket, where I put my recommendation letter.

"How long have you been volunteering at the
shelter?" I ask.

"For about a year—ever since I turned sixteen."

"Sixteen?"

"Yes," Leah says. "You have to be sixteen or
older to volunteer here."

"What if you have experience," I say, "but
you're not sixteen yet?"

"Then you have to wait. How old are you?"

"Twelve," I say, and zip my backpack pocket
closed again.

"Bummer," Leah says. "That's a long time to
wait."

"Yeah," I say.

Sophie and I thank Leah and let ourselves out of
the room because Leah is still inside the enclosure,
petting the rabbits. Sophie presses her nose against
the window to the small animal room.

"Bye, Leah. Bye, Lolli. Bye, Sunshine," she says.

Leah waves and smiles.

"Are you sure we can't take Lolli home?" Sophie
asks. "Cuddles would like her."

"No, Sophie. One rabbit is expensive enough for
now," I say. Gee, I'm starting to sound like Mom.

Sophie is disappointed we can't bring Lolli

home, and I'm so disappointed about not being able to volunteer there until I'm sixteen that I almost forget to stop at the pet store.

"Hey," Sophie says. "Don't forget, we need a new water bottle for Cuddles."

"Right," I say.

The glass water bottles at the pet store cost twice as much as the plastic ones, so I buy just one instead of the two I had planned on. Cuddles better not break this one.

We look at the rabbit toys and chew sticks, but since I'm spending so much on the water bottle, I decide to try some of Leah's strategies to entertain Cuddles instead. Maybe Cuddles will like a phone book.

It's a long walk back. We stop briefly at the park to rest. Sophie's so tired that we just sit on a bench, watching other kids play. I don't know what Sophie is thinking, but I'm thinking I have to get Josh to go with me to make an appointment for Cuddles to get spayed at Dr. Mac's. I'll ask him as soon as we get home. With any luck Maggie will still be at basketball practice like she was yesterday afternoon.

"Come on, Sophie," I say. "Time to go home and set up Cuddles's new water bottle and get her some new things to play with."

Chapter Twelve

• • • • • • • • • • •

When we get home, we find Mom painting roses on a WELCOME TO WRENCHES & ROSES sign at the kitchen table. Mom's brown hair is pulled back in a ponytail, and she's got pink and green paint smudged on one cheek.

"Cool sign," I say. I give her a kiss on her clean cheek.

I'm thinking I'll have to bribe Josh somehow to convince him to go with me to Dr. Mac's. Now would be a perfect time, because Mom looks happily busy.

"Where's Josh?" I ask.

"David called, and Josh went to visit him down

the street," she says. "It's nice to see him making friends right away."

"I don't know how he does it," I say.

Mom sets down her brush and gives me a hug.

I melt in her arms. I want to tell her how tough this has all been, but she's got enough worries with the store. So I just say, "Thanks, Mom. I needed that hug."

"Me too, sweetie, me too," she says. Then she pulls away and dabs at my chin with a napkin. "Oopsie, I didn't mean to get paint on you."

"Do you know when Josh will be back?" I ask.

"I told him to be home by six thirty—in time for dinner."

Six thirty! Too late. Dr. Mac's clinic closes at six o'clock. And when we were there yesterday at five forty-five, Dr. Mac said Maggie would be home any minute. I'd love to peek in on the tiny kittens if they're still there, but if I want to avoid Maggie, maybe I could just call to make the appointment? Then Josh could take Cuddles in to be spayed, and I can avoid Maggie and the clinic altogether.

Back in my room, I carefully take Cuddles out of her cage and let her hop around with Sophie watching her. Meanwhile, I set up Cuddles's new water bottle and clean out the wet cardboard and newspapers from her cracked and dripping old bottle.

"Don't let her chew on anything, or tell me if she starts," I say.

"Okay," says Sophie, grinning her biggest smile and happily petting Cuddles. Cuddles looks calm and happy, too, so I take the opportunity to make my call to Dr. Mac's in the hallway—away from both Mom and Sophie. I punch in the number from the free spay coupon and hope that Maggie is still at practice and won't answer the phone. I downright dread hearing her voice. If she answers, I'll just hang up. I hold my breath while it rings—three, four, five times.

"Dr. Mac's Veterinary Clinic," a friendly voice says on the other end of the line. "This is Sunita speaking. How may I help you?"

"Sunita?" I say, finally taking a breath. I'm so relieved it's her and not Maggie. "It's me, Jules. From school, with Chewie, the rabbit from Mr. Hart's class."

"Of course I remember you, Jules!" Sunita says. "Is Chewie okay?"

"Oh yes, she's fine. I just want to make an appointment with Dr. Mac to have her spayed. Mr. Hart gave me a coupon and said she was old enough now, so I should get her spayed as soon as possible."

"Okay," Sunita says. "But Dr. Mac will want to do a quick checkup a day or two before she does any surgery, and we'll need to set up a file for Chewie. I can do that for you over the phone if you want. Then I'll check with Dr. Mac to see when her next available appointment and scheduled surgery days are."

"Okay," I say. "But we changed Chewie's name to Cuddles, so could you please set up her file as Cuddles?"

"Cuddles, what a cute name!" Sunita says. Then she takes down all my info and my parents' info, too.

"Okay," Sunita says, "let me check with Dr. Mac." She puts me on hold, with first a silly duck song playing in the background, then the one about the farmer and his dog.

She's back on the line a few minutes later. "Guess what?" Sunita says. "David just arrived to help feed the abandoned kittens, and your brother is with him."

"Really?"

"Yes, and the tiny kittens are so sweet. Oh, and we had a cancellation at five fifteen today. Dr. Mac says you can bring Chew—I mean Cuddles, by for her presurgery checkup then if you want. You live nearby, right?"

"Yes, I'm just down the street," I say. "Is there anyone else there?"

"Just Dr. Gabe. He's another vet, but he's all booked up. You'll see Dr. Mac."

I look at the clock. "Okay," I say. "Thanks, Sunita. I'll be right over with Cuddles."

I hang up and tell Mom my plans.

"Jules, I'm glad you're being a responsible pet owner," Mom says. "But next time please tell me first before you make any appointments, all right? How much will a checkup cost?"

"Mr. Hart gave me a free coupon to get Cuddles spayed," I say. "And I think the presurgery check-up is part of the free coupon."

"Well," Mom says, "I'd like to go with you, but I need to finish this sign and clean up before dinner."

"I can handle it," I say. "I can carry Cuddles in her cage and ask any important questions."

"All right," Mom says. "Give me a call if anything comes up."

"I will," I say. With any luck, Cuddles can have her checkup, and I can see the kittens and get out of there before Maggie arrives.

Chapter Thirteen

· · · · · · · · · · ·

I convince Sophie to stay home and decorate a cardboard box for Cuddles.

"When I get back," I tell her, "I'll cut out some windows and doors. I saw some cardboard tubes in the store we could use for tunnels. But you can draw the door and window lines and color some parts in while I'm gone. Use these water-based markers because they're nontoxic. Don't use anything else. It might not be safe for Cuddles to chew."

Sophie reluctantly agrees, tells Cuddles goodbye, and starts to decorate the box.

I carefully scoop up Cuddles, put her in her cage, and latch the door. Then I head down the street to Dr. Mac, Sunita, David, Josh, those adorable tiny kittens, and hopefully *not* Maggie.

The bell jangles when I enter, and there is Sunita, smiling behind the desk with the big old orange tabby seemingly on guard duty next to her.

"Hi, Jules," she says to me, and then she gently pets and lifts the big cat. "Down you go, Socrates," she says as she puts him on the floor. "Now we have room for Cuddles." Sunita pats the counter for the cage.

"Okay, if you could just check over Cuddles's new file I set up and make sure all the info is correct, I'll tell Dr. Mac you're here," Sunita says. "And then do you want to see the kittens?"

"Yes, please." I check over the file, then I follow Sunita. The kittens are in the Dolittle Room again, and so are Josh, David, and a handsome man whose name tag says DR. GABE. Each of them is feeding a tiny towel-wrapped kitten from a little bottle. Three kittens suck their bottles, and two are in the box, mewing.

Everyone says hi. Sunita introduces me to Dr. Gabe, who looks right at me, steps forward, and shakes my hand. I was expecting Dr. Gabe to be an older man, not this tall, cute guy, much younger than Dr. Mac. Dr. Gabe's hand is warm and strong, and I just keep shaking it, staring at his blue, blue eyes. He smiles at me, and I can't seem to let go or stop shaking hands.

Luckily, one of the kittens mews and that brings me back to my senses. I drop my hands and hold them behind my back. I can't believe Josh gets to feed one of the kittens. Of course he is good with animals, but I can't help feeling jealous. I don't know if he's an official Vet Volunteer, but I know I'm not. And here he is, looking totally at home, like he's having a good time with David.

David's kitten is done with the bottle now and after he holds it up to burp it, he shows Josh how to swab at its rear end with a wet cotton ball to "help it learn how to pee and poop. The mother cat usually does this, really," he says, making a goofy face.

David's making jokes about how he's an "elimination expert" now. "Just call me the Prince of Poop. I know, I know, it's a thankless job, teaching kittens how to poop and pee, but someone's got to do it. The Prince of Poop to the rescue, with his sidekick Josh, the Duke of Doody!"

Sunita rolls her eyes and says she'll be right back once she knows which room Dr. Mac wants to examine Cuddles in. While she's gone, I look at the clock and wonder what time Maggie will get back. I feel out of place, especially worrying what Maggie will say if she sees me here.

Sunita pops her head back in a few minutes later. "Okay, Dr. Mac is ready in the Herriot Room," she says.

Josh nods his head to me, silently reminding me to smile with a fake smile of his own. David sets down his cotton ball and gently waves the kitty's paw at me. "Poo-bye!" David says, wiggling his nose. "Smell you later."

Sunita helps me with Cuddles's cage and shows us to the Herriot Room.

"Hello, Jules," Dr. Mac says. She looks at the chart. "And this must be Cuddles. Oh, we're going to need your mom's or dad's signature before we go much further."

"I have a coupon," I say. "Mr. Hart gave it to me."

"The coupon is fine," Dr. Mac says. "We just need an adult to sign the consent for veterinary care form." She holds up a page. "I don't suppose one of your parents could drop by?"

"Um, they're both kind of busy today. But I can bring it home and have them sign it, then bring it back the day we have Cuddles spayed," I say.

"Well, it'd be better if it were signed even before our checkup today. You live nearby, right? Sunita can keep an eye on Cuddles here if you wouldn't mind running home to get it signed. Then we can proceed. I'll just look in on my next patient while you're gone."

"Okay," I say, even though I'm thinking, *No, no, no*. What if Maggie returns?

I take the form and say, "I'll be right back." Then I head out the door, looking at the clock. Five twenty-five.

I run home. Five thirty.

Mom signs the form at five thirty-two.

I run back.

Five thirty-seven.

The door jangles as usual when I enter the clinic. But Sunita is nowhere to be found. The doors to the Dolittle Room and the Herriot Room are both closed. Even Socrates, the big orange cat, is gone.

"Hello?" I call. "Sunita? Josh? Dr. Mac?" I guess I should just go knock on the door of the Herriot Room, where I last saw Sunita and Cuddles. But what if Sunita moved Cuddles to another exam room? What if Dr. Mac is seeing a different patient in the Herriot Room? I don't want to interrupt.

Then I see the big old friendly basset hound lumbering out of the side door. He wags his tail and sniffs at me. "Hey there, Sherlock," I say, leaning down to pet him. "Where is everybody?"

I sit in one of the chairs to wait for Sunita or whoever comes out first. Sherlock leans against me and wags his tail. I pet him while I wait and look over the consent form one more time. Mom signed it just fine, but oops, no one filled in our address. I walk to the counter where I saw Sunita with a pen earlier. Sherlock trots behind me.

"I know there was a pen here," I tell Sherlock. I lean over the counter and peek in the open drawer. Yep, pens, paper clips, and uh-oh, an open cash box. They shouldn't keep cash out in the open like that. I grab a pen and reach over to close the drawer.

The front door jangles behind me. I turn, and it's Maggie. "Hey, what are you doing? Who said you could snoop around the office?" she says.

My mouth goes dry. Now what am I supposed to do? I'm sure she thinks I'm trying to steal something. I stand and look down at Sherlock for a lack of anywhere else to look. He is still wagging his tail, but slower now as he looks back and forth between us, tilting his head, puzzled.

"Come," Maggie says to Sherlock. He trots over to her and rubs his head against her leg.

"I can explain," I say. "I was just looking for a pen."

"A pen?" Maggie repeats.

"Yes. I have an appointment with Dr. Mac," I say. "A checkup for my rabbit." I look around, but of course Cuddles and Sunita are still nowhere to be seen. Maggie looks, too, as if she doesn't believe me, as if she thinks I'm there only to steal stuff and bother her.

"Listen," I say, "I know we started off on the wrong foot on the bus and in the hallway at school, not to mention in gym class, and I'm sorry about all that, but that doesn't mean—"

Maggie sighs a big sigh. I look at Sherlock again. His ears are drooping and his tail no longer wags, as if he's been scolded for doing something wrong. Sherlock didn't do anything wrong and neither did I.

"Look," I say. "I'm here to get Dr. Mac to check my rabbit. I just needed to borrow a pen." I hold up the pen in my hand.

"Fine, get your rabbit taken care of, and then go. And in the future, could you please just stay away from me, my pets, and our office drawers?" Maggie says. "Come on, Sherlock." Sherlock follows her into the side room.

Wow, I've never had anyone dislike and distrust me so much before. Ignore me, yes. Not invite me over, yes. Talk about me behind my back, yes. But out and out tell me to stay away from them? No, that's never happened before. I feel rotten.

I take a deep breath and try to recover before anyone sees me. But the door jangles again and a girl with a crow on her shoulder walks into the office.

"Hi," she says. "You're one of the new twins, right? I'm Brenna Lake."

This must be the Save-Our-Streams Brenna whom Sunita was talking about.

"Hi, I'm Jules," I say. "Jules Darrow. I like your bird. What's his name?"

"Edgar Allan Poe Crow," she says, as if it's perfectly normal to have a crow on your shoulder. The crow tilts his head and looks at me, as if he thinks I'm a curious creature, too. "Where is everybody?" Brenna asks.

"I think they're in the exam rooms," I say. "I wasn't sure if I should knock or not, so I'm just waiting."

A horn honks outside.

"Well, I can't stay," Brenna says. "My mom is waiting. I just came to drop off these flyers for our Stream Cleanup Day this Saturday. I hope you can come."

"I'd like to," I say.

"Great. We're starting at nine in the morning. Everyone's meeting at the wooden bridge behind

Quinn's horse stables. Wear boots and bring work gloves."

"I'll be there!"

"Perfect. And please come to the school library at lunchtime on Thursday," Brenna says. "I'll explain the cleanup in more detail then. We need all the help we can get." Brenna smiles a little mischievously now and adjusts her long dark hair behind her ear. "And bring your adorable brother, too. Everyone's talking about him."

The horn honks again.

"Gotta go." She opens the door. "Can you give these flyers to Dr. Mac? Or ask Maggie to tape a flyer in the window for me? I have to run." And with that, Brenna and Edgar Allan Poe Crow are right back out the door.

Sunita emerges from the Herriot Room. "I heard the door. Who was here?"

"Brenna," I say, walking away from the waiting room and the open side door, toward Sunita. "She dropped off some flyers for Stream Cleanup Day. She asked if you could tape one in the window." I figure asking Sunita is better than trying to talk to Maggie.

"Of course," Sunita says. "Did you get the consent form signed? Dr. Mac is ready for you and Cuddles. Come on in."

Chapter Fourteen

• • • • • • • • • • •

Dr. Mac makes me nervous, being Maggie's grandmother and all. Especially after Maggie thinks I
was snooping around their office cash box. I'm
glad that Sunita is here, too.

"Thanks for getting your mom's signature on
the consent form," Dr. Mac says.

"Sure," I say.

"Hello there, Cuddles," she says. Then she asks
me to take Cuddles out of her cage.

I put Cuddles on the exam table, which is covered with a towel.

"I like the way you carry her, Jules. Rabbits like
to be supported and held close like that."

Soon Dr. Mac puts me at ease, too. She is great

with Cuddles. She begins her exam, looking at Cuddles's eyes and in her ears as she talks.

"Cuddles's eyes are bright and clear. No discharge or inflamed eye tissue. Her fur is soft and shiny. Both are a good signs she's healthy. I see no skin irritations or fur mites." Dr. Mac looks up and tells me, "Rabbits shed their fur a few times each year, so be sure to brush her periodically."

"I did last night," I say.

"Great," says Dr. Mac. She uses a small light to look in Cuddles's ears. "No ear mites, dirt, or waxy buildup," she says.

"What if her ears do get wax?" I ask.

"As long as there is no dark crusty material, which could indicate mites, she should be fine. If her ears are just a little dirty, you can use gauze or cotton dipped in warm water to gently wipe them out. Rabbits are very good at grooming themselves most of the time."

She checks Cuddles's nose and chin next. "Her nose is clear, that's good," she says. "Some rabbits are prone to snuffles and other respiratory infections, so keep an eye out for sneezing and a runny nose. And don't use clay cat litter in her litter box. Some rabbits like to eat it, and that can really harm them. I see you're using shredded newspaper. Just be sure it's soy-based ink. That's fine."

"That's what Mr. Hart used," I say.

"Mr. Hart, the middle school science teacher?" Dr. Mac asks. "I thought Cuddles looked familiar."

"Her name used to be Chewie," I say. "Mr. Hart is letting my family and me adopt her because she doesn't like living in a classroom with so many students."

"I see," Dr. Mac says. "I think we might already have a file on Cuddles, formerly known as Chewie. Sunita, let's check after the exam and we can combine the two files."

"Okay," Sunita says.

Dr. Mac tells me about how rabbits have a scent gland under their chins, then she pulls Cuddles's upper and lower lips back to check her teeth and gums. "Her teeth look good, too," she says. "Be sure she gets lots of timothy hay every day and hard things to chew because rabbits' teeth are constantly growing, and they need to chew to wear them down. If her teeth get too long, it could cause serious problems, like making it difficult for her to eat. So far, everything looks a-okay."

Sunita smiles. Cuddles does not seem to mind being examined by Dr. Mac, and I am glad the vet is so thorough. Next she looks at each of Cuddles's paws and legs. "I'm glad you put a sheet of wood covered with changeable cardboard in the bottom of her cage," Dr. Mac says, "and you're using a lit-ter box instead of just a wire-bottomed cage with a litter pan below."

"Mr. Hart set it up that way," I say.

"Good idea to keep using that technique, espe-cially if Cuddles likes to use her litter box," she says. "Rabbits are prone to sore feet and possible infection if they have to sit on wire caging all day."

I'm glad Mr. Hart put the wood in the bottom of her cage.

"Cuddles's nails are a little long," Dr. Mac says. "Sunita, clippers, please."

Sunita hands her the small clippers, and Dr. Mac trims the nails on one of Cuddles's front feet. "Rabbits in the wild wear down their nails natural-ly, but pet rabbits need their nails trimmed periodi-cally so they don't get too long, become ingrown, or cause injury if they catch on something."

"How often should I trim her nails?" I ask.

"Oh, about once a month should do it. Come closer, I'll show you how." Dr. Mac shows me how to hold each paw to extend the nails. "Just trim the white part of the nail, like I'm doing," Dr. Mac says. "Not the pink part. That's the quick, and it contains the nerve and blood supply."

"Okay, your turn, Jules." Dr. Mac hands me the clippers and nods as I give it a try.

"I used to help trim the cats' nails at the shelter in Pittsburgh," I say.

"That's it," she says. "Looks like you know what you're doing. Best to trim just a little each time, like you're doing."

Dr. Mac checks Cuddles all over. "Feeling for any lumps or bumps," she says. Then she turns her over on her arm and looks at her belly, scent glands near her bottom, and genital area. "All clean, no urine burn or caked-on feces."

I'm surprised that Cuddles is behaving so well. I guess Dr. Mac really does know animals!

Dr. Mac weighs her next and pets her. "Cuddles, you are one sweet little rabbit, and you have a clean bill of health." She looks up at me and smiles. "Do you have any questions, Jules?"

"What happens when she is spayed? Will it hurt her?"

"We'll use a combination of premedication and gas anesthesia so she will be relaxed and won't be in any discomfort during the surgery. We'll shave her abdomen and wash her with a skin disinfectant. Afterward she'll feel a little tender while she heals and may want to hide away a bit more than usual. Just make sure that she begins to eat and drink within twenty-four hours. Rabbits have a sensitive digestive system and need to keep a balance of good bacteria in it. So they need to eat and digest right away."

"When will her surgery be? And will she have to stay here overnight?" I ask.

"I can do the surgery Friday. Can you bring her here Friday morning before you go to school?"

"Yes," I say, petting Cuddles. I hope Dad or Josh or Mom can come with me.

"I can perform her surgery in the morning. She'll be a little groggy afterward, but post-op we will keep her warm and comfortable and she will be fine in a few hours. As long as you can create a calm, quiet atmosphere for her to recuperate in at home, she can go home with you later Friday afternoon."

"Is it okay for her to eat before the surgery?"

"Yes, give her food and water as usual. Rabbits cannot vomit like other animals."

"They can't?" I ask.

Even Sunita looks surprised.

"That's right," Dr. Mac says. "Because rabbits can't vomit, there is no reason to withhold food and water. Remember, it's important to watch her after surgery to make sure that she is eating, drinking, and eliminating."

"Are you sure she'll be okay?" I ask. All of a sudden, Cuddles looks so small and vulnerable sitting there on the big towel atop the metal exam table.

Dr. Mac nods. "I know it's hard not to worry, but I've spayed rabbits many times, always with a good outcome. Cuddles should be just fine in a day or two."

Sunita says, "She's in good hands with Dr. Mac."

"Okay," I say. "I'll bring her in Friday morning before school."

Sunita walks with me as I bring Cuddles's cage back to the waiting room, where Josh and David are hanging out.

"All done?" Josh asks. "Everything okay with Cuddles?"

"Yes," I say. "Thanks again, Sunita."

"You're welcome," she says.

"You guys going?" David asks. "I'll walk with you."

"Wait for me, too," Sunita says. "I just have to hang up this flyer for Stream Cleanup Day. Are you going?"

"Oh yeah," David says. "I wouldn't miss it. Plus, they're planning a barbecue lunch afterward. Hello, roasted hot dogs. I'll be there."

"Bye, Dr. Mac," Sunita calls out. "We're all leaving."

Dr. Mac comes out of the Dolittle Room to say good-bye. "Thanks, Sunita, thanks, David. The kittens look great. You too, Josh. Thanks."

I wish I could have helped out with the kittens, too. "Hey, Josh," David says as we exit the clinic. "Do you want to bike to the stables with me on Saturday morning before Stream Cleanup? I'm sure we can find you an extra pair of boots there, too, if you need them."

"Great," Josh says. "Thanks. Count me in."

Sunita's mom is there to pick her up. She waves good-bye.

I can't even wave because I'm using both hands to carry Cuddles, so I just say, "Bye."

"You know, Josh," David says, as we walk down the street, "I could ask my mom if you could stay over Friday night and if we could set up my tent in the backyard. Have a little campout, toast some marshmallows, or whatever."

"That'd be cool," Josh says.

"Okay, then, let me ask my mom, and I'll let you know at school tomorrow," David says.

"Thanks for letting me tag along to Dr. Mac's," Josh says.

"Sure," says David. "See you tomorrow."

"See you tomorrow," Josh replies.

Great, just great. Josh has a friend and is getting invited all over the place. And he's helping Dr. Mac. He's probably already a full-fledged Vet Volunteer as far as I know. And me? I can't even volunteer at the shelter. No one is inviting me anywhere. Maggie hates me and doesn't want me anywhere near the clinic. She probably doesn't want me at Stream Cleanup Day, either. Not only that, but Brenna probably only invited me to Stream Cleanup Day so she could see my "adorable brother."

At least I have Cuddles. When I get home, I'm going to make her the best bunny castle ever, with cardboard boxes, tubes, and ramps.

* * * * *

After dinner, Sophie shows me the cardboard house she decorated with markers.

"Look," she says. "I drew carrots and a rainbow and me! And here is Cuddles hopping. And I drew her sleeping. See, her eyes are closed. And here she is pooping. Ha. Ha. Ha. See the poop?"

"Nice job, Sophie," I say. It's true that Cuddles poops a lot. Luckily, she uses her litter box, so the cleanup is easy. I cut doors and windows in the box and add a round hole to poke through the long cardboard tube I found earlier in the store. Josh and Sophie bring me more empty boxes from our move.

When Mom is out of the room, Josh empties a container of oatmeal into a plastic bag and brings me the empty cylindrical oats container. "Here's another tunnel or hidey hole," he says. I begin assembly in our room with Cuddles watching curiously from her cage.

Josh hangs out in our room, giving me all kinds of advice. "Put that ramp on the other side."

An hour later, Cuddles has the best Cuddles Castle ever, if I do say so myself. And she loves it. She's out of her cage, sniffing and exploring her many-roomed, odd-looking cardboard castle. It has plenty of openings, ramps, tunnels, hidey holes, and peekaboo windows.

"She's peeking out the window." Sophie giggles. "Look, look, now she's on top of her castle!"

Cuddles is so cute hopping all over and around her castle, through the tunnels and windows, and poking her head in and out. Josh is stretched out on the floor, encouraging and petting her. Cuddles is too happy and curious to sit still for much petting. Sophie lies on my bed laughing and clapping. I sit on the floor nearby to make sure Cuddles does not chew on any books or cords or anything bad, but she is so busy, she forgets all about chewing the wrong things. Leah at the shelter was right about bored bunnies. I'm glad she gave me so many ideas for easy, safe activities to keep Cuddles active and happy. Plus, Cuddles is so much funnier and friskier than she used to be.

"Funny bunny, funny bunny!" Sophie laughs.

Mom knocks on the door and pokes her head in. "Sounds like I'm missing all the fun," she says. "What's all the giggling about?" She looks at Sophie laughing at Cuddles's silliness. Mom is smiling now, too, standing inside the closed door so Cuddles doesn't escape. "My, what a snazzy dream house she has."

"Yeah," Josh says. "Jules has a future in bunny architecture."

"I think you're right," Mom says. "And speaking of your future, does anyone have any homework?"

"Just a little," Josh says. "I'll do it in here."

"Me too," Sophie and I say in unison.

And we do, while Cuddles hops around exploring. She finally flops down on her side next to me and lets me pet her. Mom has already left, and I wish she could see how sweet Cuddles is when she's had plenty of exercise, but I don't want to disturb or move her. So I just pet her and I'm so happy that she's content. Tomorrow I'll look for a phone book and some other things to keep her occupied. But for now—all is well. Mom seems to like Cuddles. Just a few more days and she will be convinced that Cuddles can stay. Maybe moving to Ambler will turn out okay after all.

Chapter Fifteen

. . . .

On Thursday, I still try to avoid Maggie on the bus ride to school. Josh is best buddies with David now, so my former strategy of sitting with my twin is shot. Josh jabbers away with David as we get on the bus, then they both pretty much forget all about me. So I sit by myself behind the bus driver. I wish Sunita took the same bus to school.

At lunch I go to the library for Brenna's Save Our Streams meeting. The library is so packed with people, students are sitting on the tables and floor. It's way too crowded, so I have to stand in the back. Mr. Hart calls the meeting to order and says that the whole school will be studying ecology and water systems in the next month. Then he introduces Brenna Lake.

Everyone claps. I hear David off to the side making some dumb joke about why Brenna *Lake* is cleaning up a stream and not a lake. David gets a few chuckles, but most everyone, including Brenna, ignores him. Brenna asks for the lights to be turned down and shows slides of all kinds of local wildlife at the Gold Hill Nature Preserve, where she lives with her family. The lights come back on, and she stands at the podium and asks the students to help out at the community-wide Save Our Streams Cleanup Day on Saturday.

"Last year we had over fifty volunteers," Brenna says. "In just half a day, we collected fifty-seven bags of trash, three tires, various car parts, and an old washing machine out of the stream. This year we hope to at least double the number of volunteers and clean up an even longer stretch of stream. We'll sort the junk we collect from the stream and recycle all the plastic, glass, metal, and aluminum. We really want to get the message out to keep our streams clean. Here's why."

Brenna holds up a big photo of a duck with its neck stuck in a plastic six-pack ring. It's hard to look at. Next she shows a beaver tangled in fishing line and a baby raccoon with its head stuck in a dirty glass jar. It makes me feel sick to my stomach to see these injured animals. I'm not the only one who feels that way. There are gasps and silence.

"At the wildlife center, we see so many injured animals. Birds and foxes and other animals end up eating all kinds of dangerous things that people have left behind. Like the defenseless little raccoon I showed you with its head stuck in a jar. They can't get themselves free, and sometimes they die of starvation. Innocent animals are trapped, injured, suffocate, and die because of plastic bags, fishing line, and plastic six-pack rings. I've seen birds and mammals with cuts on their feet from broken glass. It has to stop. Our local wildlife is depending on us for clean, safe, and unpolluted water. So who can help us clean the stream this Saturday?"

Everyone's hand goes up, including mine.

"Great," Brenna says. "Stream Cleanup Day is just a beginning. When we're done for the day, we'll report back in the newspaper and on our new blog to make people aware of recycling and how to prevent polluting our streams."

Wow, she has it all planned out.

"I have sign-up sheets for general volunteers, sorters, photographers, and reporters. And we're still looking for businesses to donate snacks and drinks. Can anyone think of anything else we need?"

Before I realize what I'm doing, my hand shoots up and Brenna nods to me. "Yes?" she asks.

I hate speaking in front of big groups of people. But this is important. "It sounds like you are going to need lots of garbage bags," I stammer.

"Yes," Brenna says. "In fact, last year we ran out and were scrambling at the last minute."

"Well, what if each of us brings some garbage bags from home and we ask our neighbors and local businesses to donate, too? I bet my parents would donate some from their store."

"Great idea, Jules!" Brenna says, and writes it down on her notepad. "Who thinks they can bring bags, and who wants to try to ask some local businesses to donate?"

More kids raise their hands, and Brenna writes down their names. I'm surprised at myself for raising my hand and speaking up in such a large group, but proud that Brenna liked my idea.

And now I know Brenna didn't just invite me because she thinks Josh is cute. It sounds like she needs a lot of help. Plus, it sounds fun. I'll ask Dad if the store can donate some garbage bags and maybe help with other recycling plans.

"We start at nine o'clock Saturday morning,"

Brenna shouts out over everyone's excitement. "Wear boots or waders and gloves," she says. "Please take more flyers with you and tell your neighbors, families, and friends."

So far Sunita is my only potential friend, and she already knows about Stream Cleanup Day. But I take a few flyers anyway and sign up as a general volunteer. I set the clipboard down. I want to talk to Brenna and tell her how excited I am to participate, but she is surrounded by other kids wanting to talk to her, too.

I wait a few minutes and finally get closer to the desk where she has her photos, notes, and more clipboards. There are more sign-up sheets with all the slots filled. And on the top of another page of "GENERAL VOLUNTEERS" in bright blue letters is the name Maggie MacKenzie. My stomach flip-flops. At first I think of switching to another job or not going to Stream Cleanup Day at all, but I refuse to be afraid of Maggie. Maybe she doesn't want me anywhere near her grandma's clinic, but she can't keep me from going to the stream, helping animals, and making new friends like Brenna and Sunita.

Finally it's my turn to talk to Brenna. "Hi again," I say, kind of nervous, but determined. "I just want to tell you I'm behind you one hundred percent. I'll be there on Saturday. If you need help with anything else before then, just call. My phone number is on the sign-up."

"Great," Brenna says. "Thanks for getting involved. I'll see you on Saturday."

• • • • • •

After school, Josh takes off for David's house. I'm so happy I got through the day without any more incidents with Maggie. We played basketball in gym again, but thankfully she and I ended up on different teams and played in different games.

At home, I check on Cuddles, pet her, and feed her some greens and apples. She loves apple slices. Sophie wants to help, too, filling the water bottle, making sure Cuddles is safe while I clean the cage, and feeding her more apple slices. Sophie also wants to pick up Cuddles and carry her back to the cage, but I tell her that's my job. Instead, I show her how to latch the cage shut so Cuddles can't get out. That seems to satisfy Sophie for now.

Sophie goes to the kitchen to do her homework with Mom. Dad comes in and says, "I've got another shipment coming in after the weekend, and I need to make room for more stock. I'm ready to tackle the basement cleanup, but I need some helpers. Any volunteers?"

Josh and I both chip in. The basement is huge,

and I can't wait until we have it all cleaned up so we can set up a family workshop down there.

Josh and I take armful after armful of cardboard boxes to the recycling bin behind the store. Before I dump each load, I scrounge around a bit for anything that would make interesting additions to Cuddles's castle. I also check for the stray tabby in the alley behind the store, but there is no sign of him. We're probably making too much noise.

Dad lets me hang a flyer for Stream Cleanup Day in the store window, even though the store won't open for another two weeks. He says he'd be happy to donate garbage bags and maybe he'll even have time to volunteer on Saturday morning.

"It'd be a good way to help out and get to know members of the community," Dad says. I agree— it'll be great to have Dad there, especially if Josh is hanging out with David and ignoring me.

After dinner, Josh is in our room again. Sophie decorates the outside walls of Cuddles's castle with more flowers and butterflies. Sophie is a little calmer today and so is Cuddles. Even Josh notices.

"Cuddles is not only behaving herself," he whispers to me, "but your newly tamed rabbit is going to help tame our sister, too. Sophie will be easier to babysit now that we have Cuddles to distract and entertain her."

"I know," I reply. "Did I tell you Mr. Hart called me the bunny whisperer? Because no one else had been able to pet Cuddles."

Josh laughs. "Yep, you're the bunny whisperer all right. What have I been telling you? You have a sixth sense."

Josh commenting on my Animal Sense makes me feel good. He sits at my desk and watches as I add another cardboard room with rounded windows and doors to Cuddles's castle. I use Sophie's markers and write CUDDLES above the biggest door in fancy lettering.

Cuddles goes from calm to frisky again, hopping around exploring her new addition, stopping to groom her face and whiskers, then energetically sniffing and hopping again. I didn't find a phone book yet, but Cuddles loves the toilet paper roll I made her with a carrot inside and a little hay stuck in both ends. She is so adorable and funny, chewing and throwing the cardboard roll around until she finally gets the carrot inside. Sophie keeps drawing tons of pictures of Cuddles doing all kinds of things and hanging them in our room. Hopping, hiding, exploring, sleeping, sniffing, and pooping.

"You've got quite a gallery of bunny art, Sophie," Josh says, studying all her drawings.

"I know," she says, beaming a Sophie-sized smile. "I'm an artist."

Cuddles does a funny hop and high leap that looks makes her look like she's dancing.

I'm so glad we got her. Josh and Sophie are, too. And so far, no complaints from Mom or Dad. I think we'll complete our one-week trial period no problem.

• • • • •

Friday morning I wake up early. I make sure Cuddles eats, then I clean out her cage and wait for Josh to finish breakfast. It's time to take Cuddles to Dr. Mac's, and I'm glad Josh has agreed to go with me. When we get to Dr. Mac's, the door is still locked, so Josh rings the after-hours bell. Through the glass door we see Sherlock lumber out through the side door, followed by Dr. Mac. She unlocks the door.

"Good morning, everyone," Dr. Mac says. "Thanks for bringing Cuddles by bright and early." The vet looks a little tired.

"I hope we didn't make you get up too early," Josh says.

"Oh no, we were up early feeding hungry kittens!" Dr. Mac laughs. "In fact, Maggie is still feeding the last one now."

Dr. Mac asks a couple of quick questions about how Cuddles is feeling and when she last ate, then tells us she'll do the spay later in the morning, "When Dr. Gabe is here to help hold down the fort. You can come by after school. Cuddles should be sufficiently recovered by then, and you can take her home to rest up."

"Okay," Josh says.

"See you soon, Cuddles. Be good," I say. My throat tightens as I open the latch on the cage and pet her before we go. "Will she be okay?" I ask Dr. Mac.

Dr. Mac nods, and Josh grabs my arm.

"Come on, Jules," he says. "Cuddles will be fine. We don't want to miss the bus. Let's go."

"Don't worry," Dr. Mac says. "You'll see Cuddles right after school." Then she heads down the hall toward the Dolittle Room, carrying Cuddles in her cage. Cuddles looks at me as if she is saying, *Wait? Where am I going?* She looks smaller and smaller as she is carried away down the hall.

"Maggie," Dr. Mac calls out. "Grab your stuff. You're going to be late for the bus again!"

"Let's go," I tell Josh. And we walk quickly to the bus stop.

Chapter Sixteen

. . . .

I know that Dr. Mac is a great veterinarian and that she told me not to worry. But I can't help wondering about how Cuddles is doing. I worry during science class, looking at the empty spot where her cage used to be. I can barely eat during lunch because I'm still worrying. So instead, I go to the library and look up rabbit spaying on the Internet. Most of the links just say how good it is to have your rabbit spayed. But a few of them describe complications. So I worry the rest of the day and the entire bus ride home. I can't wait to get to the clinic.

David gets off the bus with Josh and me. "I promised Dr. Mac I'd help feed the kittens after school today," David tells Josh. "Do you want to come?"

"Sure," Josh says. "Jules is heading over to pick up Cuddles, anyway. I just need to go home first and tell my parents. I can meet you there in about twenty minutes."

"Great," says David. "I'll drop my stuff at home, too. See you there."

Josh and I head home.

Mom wants us to wash up and eat a snack before we head back to Dr. Mac's, but I'm so nervous about Cuddles, I can barely eat. I hope she's okay.

Dad comes with Josh and me, while Sophie stays at home with Mom.

"I'll decorate her house some more," Sophie says. "And make her a welcome home sign."

When we arrive, Josh heads off to find David. Dr. Mac is with another patient, so Dr. Gabe takes Dad and me to see Cuddles in the recovery room, a quiet, dimly lit room with other cages—mostly big cages for cats and dogs. Cuddles looks so tiny and alone.

"Hey there, Cuddles," I say. I open the latch to pet her through the top of the cage. But she moves away from my hand and crouches down in the back corner of the cage. "Is she okay?" I ask Dr. Gabe.

"Yes, the surgery went fine. No problems. She might be a little more cautious for a day or two as she recuperates."

Dad says, "Thank you," and shakes Dr. Gabe's hand. Then he squats down next to me to look at Cuddles.

"Dr. Mac will be out in a minute to tell you more about postsurgery care." Dr. Gabe says.

Dad's cell phone rings. He goes outside to answer it so he won't disturb the animals.

"May I stay here with Cuddles?" I ask.

"Of course," Dr. Gabe says.

"Thanks." I sit on the floor outside Cuddles's cage. "I'm here, Cuddles," I say. She stays very still. She doesn't approach me or look at me at all.

Dr. Mac enters the recovery room and squats down beside me. She listens to Cuddles with her stethoscope.

"Cuddles is doing just fine, Jules. The incision site might be sensitive, so be very gentle and try not to let her hop around too much. And be sure she eats and drinks. It's important to keep a rabbit's digestive system moving. She doesn't look at ease here with the cats and dogs in recovery, so I think she'll be happier at home."

"Okay," I say, happy I can bring her home but nervous, too. "Do I need to do anything?"

"Just keep her calm and quiet," Dr. Mac says. "And try to get her to eat a little tonight if you can. The sooner she eats, the better."

Dr. Mac lifts Cuddles carefully out of her cage and shows me her shaved belly, where the stitches are. "You can see, it's a little tender now, but there shouldn't be swelling or discharge. You can check her incision site once or twice a day. Keep her cage and litter box clean and that will help keep the incision clean, too."

"Should I feed her anything different?" I ask.

"No, just your usual, or, if she seems reluctant to eat, give her any treats she likes," Dr. Mac says.

"She loves apples and carrots," I say.

"Perfect," Dr. Mac says. "After you rinse them in water, don't dry them off. That will give Cuddles a little bit of liquid at the same time, in case she is not drinking yet. And offer her plenty of hay as well."

"I will."

"Call or bring her back if she isn't eating or using her litter box by tomorrow, if she's not her usual self in a few days, or if it looks like there is any sign of infection at the incision site. There shouldn't be, but keep an eye out just in case."

"Okay," I say. "Thanks, Dr. Mac."

Dad is still outside on the phone. I can see him

through the front window. Dr. Mac walks with me. I carry Cuddles in her cage toward the door, where we see Josh and David coming down the hall.

"Great, there you are," Dr. Mac tells them. "The kittens are mewing and very hungry."

"Kitten patrol to the rescue," says David. "I brought Josh to help."

"The more the merrier and the sooner they can eat, the better," Dr. Mac says. "Be sure the calico gets enough. She's been slower to nurse, and she isn't gaining weight like the others."

"Will do," David says.

"They're in the Dolittle Room, mewing up a storm," Dr. Mac says. "The bottles and kitten formula are there, too, all clean and ready to go. You can take it from here, right, David?"

"Sure," he says.

"All right, then. Bye, Jules. Bye, boys. I'm off to my next patient," Dr. Mac says, and she heads toward the Herriot Room.

"Jules is great with cats," Josh tells David. "It's like she has a sixth sense—Animal Sense. Can she help us feed the kittens?"

"Fine by me," David says.

"I don't know," I say. "I have to watch Cuddles."

"Just ask your dad to bring Cuddles home, or

bring Cuddles in with us," David says. "There's plenty of room for her cage on the floor. Come on, we have to get started. You can help us with poop patrol, too."

Of course I'd love to help with the kittens, but I think of Maggie telling me to stay away. And I think about Cuddles. She must be stressed enough from her surgery. I need to get her home and make sure she is calm and comfortable. I doubt she'll like being around mewing kittens right now, even though I'd sure like to be.

"No, I have to go," I say.

"Don't you even want to see them?" Josh asks.

"Oh okay," I say. "Just for a minute." I poke my head out the door and tell Dad I'll be out shortly.

"Take your time," Dad says, and goes back to his phone call.

I bring Cuddles in her cage and follow Josh and David into the room with the box full of kittens.

They are even cuter than last time. The two gray ones and the two black ones are noticeably chubbier, lifting their heads and mewing loudly. But the little calico is tinier than the rest and her mew is so much weaker.

David and Josh wash their hands, and I go closer to peek into the box. "Feed the calico first," I say. "She needs it the most."

David fills five bottles with kitten formula, and then warms them in a pot of water. "You sure you don't want to help us?" he asks.

"Oh, I do," I say, "but I've got to get home."

"Maybe next time," he says.

"Maybe," I say. I pick up Cuddles in her cage and leave the clinic, trying not to bump the cage too much.

Maybe next time. I wish I could come back when Cuddles is feeling better so I could help with those tiny kittens. But there won't be any next time. Today might be my last time at Dr. Mac's clinic before Cuddles's next checkup. Looks like Josh is well on his way to being a Vet Volunteer. But not me.

I wish I hadn't squished Maggie's project on the bus. I wish I hadn't said anything about the whole tutoring thing, or tried to "fix it" when Maggie was talking to Mr. Hart about her project. I wish that I was better at basketball and that Maggie didn't think I was a snoop—or even worse, a thief. Everything's gone from bad to worse with Maggie. It's so bad now, I can't ever be a Vet Volunteer.

Dad helps me carry Cuddles as gently as we can back home. I bring her to my room, keep the lights dim, and sit down next to her cage. She looks at me but stays hunched and still in the back of her cage.

"How are you doing, Cuddles?" I ask. "I know how you feel. Pretty rotten, huh?"

She has her hay and rabbit food to eat, but she is not touching it. She doesn't go near her water bottle, either. Dr. Mac said to try to get her to eat as soon as possible. So I leave her for a few minutes to rinse some leafy greens, carrots, and apple slices. But she won't even take the tiniest bite. Not even of her favorite, sliced apples.

She lets me pet her through the top of her cage, but it is pretty clear she does not want to come out and hop around. So I pet her, talk to her, and tell her I hope she feels better soon. I offer her more carrots and apple slices one by one, but she just turns her head and refuses to take a bite.

That night, I have a hard time going to sleep, worrying about her.

Chapter Seventeen

• • • • • • • • • • •

In the morning, I wake to the familiar sound of Cuddles sipping from her water bottle. Thank goodness. The little metal pipe makes a reassuring clicking sound as she licks it to get the water.

I'm out of bed and next to her cage. "Feeling better?" I ask in a quiet voice. "Did you eat anything?"

I look at her food bowls and my heart drops. All three bowls are still full. She hasn't touched her hay, her bunny food, or the carrots and apples and greens. In fact, the apples look brown and yucky and the greens are wilted. I check her litter box and there is just a little urine and hardly any poop. The few droppings that are there are smaller than usual.

"Come on, Cuddles. I'm glad you're drinking, but you have to eat. And poop, too. Doctor's orders." I open her cage, pet her a little, remove the apples and greens, and latch her cage closed again.

Dad and I are supposed to go to Stream Cleanup Day. Josh camped out at David's last night, and they're probably riding bikes to the cleanup site already.

"All ready, Jules?" Dad asks as I enter the kitchen.

"I don't know," I say. "I think I'll stay home and watch Cuddles. She still seems a little down after her surgery."

"Oh," he says. "What's wrong?"

Mom looks up. "Something's wrong?" she asks. Is she concerned about how Cuddles is feeling, or is she concerned I might not be a responsible pet owner?

"Well, I'm doing everything Dr. Mac told me," I say. "And Cuddles is drinking her water, but she is not eating much yet." I don't say I'm worried because it looks like she hasn't eaten at all since yesterday morning.

"Didn't Dr. Mac say that's normal after surgery?" Mom asks.

"Yes, but she also said I should offer her treats and watch her to make sure she's eating and using her litter box," I say. "I don't think I should be away from her all day. Sorry, Dad, I was looking forward to cleaning up the stream with you."

"I'll go with you, Daddy!" Sophie says as she jumps into Dad's lap and grabs him tightly around his neck. Dad hugs Sophie back, but he raises his eyebrows and looks at Mom.

"Maybe I'll go, too," Mom says. "I've been stuck indoors all week getting the books set up for the store. It'll be great to be outdoors for a change. And help out with a good cause. Jules, are you sure you won't join us? Will you be okay alone?"

I nod.

"Yay! We're going to the stream." Sophie shouts, and runs to our room.

"Sophie, not so loud!" I say. "Cuddles needs calm and quiet to recuperate."

"Sorry," Sophie says, then I hear her whispering loudly to Cuddles, "Bye, Cuddles, see you later."

Soon Mom, Dad, and Sophie are racing up and down the stairs to the store, then back and forth to the car in the alley, loading up plastic bags, shovels, boots, and flyers about the grand opening of Wrenches & Roses. I'm sad I'm not going with them, but when they finally leave I'm glad the house is quiet. I bet Cuddles is, too. I wash and slice a new apple, a few sprigs of parsley, and some celery leaves and return to my room, hoping to find

Cuddles already eating her hay or bunny food.

Oh no! The latch is undone on her cage door. The cage door is completely open, and the cage is empty. Cuddles is gone!

Sophie must have unhooked the latch to pet Cuddles when she said good-bye, then left it completely open. I close the bedroom door. "Cuddles, here, Cuddles," I call. She must still be in the room. I look under the beds, behind our desks, and in the closet that Sophie left open, too. I look everywhere in our bedroom, but I can't find her. I run to the hallway. All the bedroom and bathroom doors are open, so I close them all and check the hallway, the kitchen, and the living room first. Not a trace of her. Not even a single little dropping. Now I'm really worried.

"Cuddles, Cuddles," I call again, even though she has never come when I called.

I check the bathroom and carefully search my parents' and Josh's bedrooms. I hope she doesn't chew a cord, eat something poisonous, or injure herself hopping around. Then I remember the stairs and door to the back alley. It was open when Mom, Dad, and Sophie were running up and down getting supplies for the stream cleanup. What if Cuddles got out? Could she have hopped down the stairs when no one was looking?

I should call Mom and Dad. I need help. Did they bring their cell phones? But wait. What if Mom thinks I'm a bad pet owner?

How could Sophie leave the latch open like that? *Okay, think, Jules.* When did they leave? Just five or ten minutes ago. Cuddles couldn't have gotten far.

"Cuddles, Cuddles, where are you?" I whisper. I race to the stairs and go up and down them twice, trying to decide what to do. I look out in the alley and catch my breath. I don't think she could have gotten down the stairs after being sore from her surgery. Not without anyone seeing her.

I'll never forgive Sophie if something happens to Cuddles. I'll never forgive myself. I shouldn't have shown Sophie how to open and close the latch. I should have reminded her to close it every time. I should have double-checked.

I have to keep looking. If I don't find her in five minutes, I'll call Mom and Dad.

I get the cordless phone from the kitchen. I check the clock. Back to my bedroom. That's the last place I saw her. I squat down near her cage. I have to think like a rabbit. If I were feeling sore and groggy, what would I do?

Eat? No.

Run away? No.

Hide? Yes.

I lie on the floor and try to look at everything from Cuddles's point of view. Under the beds would be good, but she's not there.

Four minutes left.

I pick up Cuddles's cardboard castle and put it on my bed. It's bulky but not very heavy so I don't expect to find Cuddles there, but I check each little hidey hole, tunnel, and room. No. No Cuddles. But oh no, maybe she was hiding there. There's a drop of blood on the cardboard floor of the castle. Fresh blood.

I carefully pick up Sophie's pajamas from the floor. No Cuddles, but another drop of blood.

Two minutes left.

I'm on my hands and knees, looking for more drops of blood. This is bad, really bad. It's so quiet, I can hear my heart thumping. Then there's a rustle in our closet. I carefully slide the closet door open, and there she is, sitting on Sophie's robe, which has fallen to the floor. She stops chewing on the fuzzy collar of the robe and looks up at me.

"Cuddles, there you are."

I am so relieved, but when I reach for her, Cuddles grunts at me and hops away. "Come on, Cuddles, it's time to rest up now. You had me so worried," I say, but Cuddles does not want to be picked up. Every time I reach for her, she hops away.

She's not as playful and as full of dancing hops as she was before she got spayed. In fact, she is slower, and she seems afraid of me. I close the closet door so she has one less place to hide. I close our bedroom door, too, and decide just to wait to see if she calms down. I put her water bottle facing the outside on her cage, and I bring her food bowls out, too, hoping she will feel hungry or thirsty after all her hopping around. I lie on my bed, talking calmly to her. And I wait.

And wait.

She finally stops hopping and rests on an extra piece of cardboard left over from her castle. I watch her from my bed. She sits very still for a moment but she seems to be panting a little. She used to hop all over the place, but I don't remember her panting at all before. I'm worried. I have to catch her and confine her to her cage so she won't exhaust herself. And I have to encourage her to eat and drink. After chasing her around the room for at least ten minutes, I realize she still hasn't peed or pooped. I move very slowly from the bed, talking to her calmly. "You're okay now, Cuddles, just let me help you into your cage."

She doesn't look happy, but she lets me scoop her up. "You're safe now," I say as I lift her carefully, supporting her rear end and chest and holding her close to my body. I can feel her heart beating very fast through her furry chest wall where I hold her.

"Don't worry, Cuddles," I say as I give her a kiss on the top of her head. "You're okay."

But I don't think she *is* okay. Her ears are super hot against my cheek. I've petted and nuzzled my cheek against her ears before and they were never this hot. I look down at the cardboard, and there is a smear of fresh blood on the cardboard where she was sitting. And not just a drop or two. Cuddles is bleeding.

I'm afraid to turn her or hold her up high to see her belly. I don't want to frighten her. Her heart still feels like it is beating too fast. But I need to see the incision site. I carefully carry her to the bathroom and stand in front of the big mirror so I can see her belly without agitating her. The site of the incision looks way worse than when Dr. Mac showed it to me yesterday afternoon. Now it looks like some of the stitches have come undone. Her skin is all puffy and swollen, and there is more blood.

I get a clean, dry washcloth to hold against the wound.

"Okay, okay, Cuddles," I say, trying to reassure her and myself at the same time. "We're going back to Dr. Mac's right away. You're going to be just fine." But I'm worried as I carry her carefully back to her cage, set her inside, and hope she'll lie down on the soft washcloth. She doesn't.

"Here, drink some water," I tell her as I re-arrange her water bottle so the spout is back inside the cage where she can reach it. "Drink some water, Cuddles," I say desperately. "I think you're too hot. It'll cool you down." But she moves away from the water and me. She crouches in the back of her cage like she did yesterday, only now she is panting, and it looks like her body is starting to shake in little tremors.

I call the clinic to tell Dr. Mac I'm bringing her in, but the phone just rings and rings. Finally an answering machine picks up stating their office hours and saying that Dr. Mac might be with a patient and to please leave a message. They're open on Saturdays, but I don't have time to leave a message. I slip on my shoes, grab Cuddles in her cage, and walk as fast as I can to Dr. Mac's, all the while trying not to jostle her too much.

"You're okay, Cuddles," I say. "I know you're going to be okay."

But really, I have no idea if she will be okay or not.

Chapter Eighteen

• • • • • • • • • • • • •

I push open the door to Dr. Mac's clinic and hear the familiar jangle of the bell above the door. The waiting room is empty. I set Cuddles's cage down.

"Hello, hello!" I call. "Is there anyone here?" I know a lot of the Vet Volunteers are at Stream Cleanup Day, but someone has to be here. The front door was unlocked after all. But even the basset hound, Sherlock, and Socrates, the cat, are missing.

I look down at Cuddles in her cage. She's biting at her stitches. "No, Cuddles," I say. I jiggle her water bottle to distract her. She stops chewing at her incision site and looks at me, then goes right back to biting at her belly.

"I need some help!" I call louder. "Dr. Mac? Dr. Gabe?" I'm panicking. I hear it in my voice.

The Dolittle Room door opens. Finally! Dr. Mac must have been with another patient. But as the door opens farther, it's not Dr. Mac who emerges. It's Maggie, holding the tiny calico kitten and a bottle of kitten formula.

"What's wrong?" Maggie asks, walking closer. Her face is full of concern, looking at Cuddles in her cage.

"Is Dr. Mac here?" I ask.

"No," Maggie says. "She just left on an emergency call—something about a baby fox trapped in some equipment they found at the stream. Is your rabbit okay?"

"No," I say. "She's pulling out her stitches from her surgery. She's bleeding, breathing rapidly, and she's shaking. What about Dr. Gabe? Is he here?"

"No," Maggie says. "He's out on call at Abbott's Farm. He won't be back for a couple of hours." Maggie leans down and looks in at Cuddles.

"You've got to help me," I say. "Please, you've got to help Cuddles."

"Follow me," Maggie says. I follow her to the Dolittle Room, and she puts the kitten back in a box with its four mewing siblings. "Bring your rabbit out here," Maggie says. "I'll take her temperature, and we'll call my grandmother. She'll tell us what to do."

Maggie washes her hands and puts on a pair of gloves. "Hey, isn't that Chewie?" she asks. "From Mr. Hart's class?"

"Yes, her name is Cuddles now."

"Better wash your hands, too," Maggie says. "Use that scrub brush. If she has an open wound, we want to avoid any germs that might cause infection." So I do, then I carefully carry Cuddles to the metal exam table, where Maggie has placed a clean towel.

"Hold her up carefully, so I can see where she's bleeding," Maggie says, "then wrap her like a bunny burrito in the towel, but leave her tail end exposed so I can take her temperature."

"Do you know what you're doing?" I ask. "Shouldn't you call Dr. Mac first?"

"Do you want my help or not?" Maggie glares at me. "I know how to take a dog's, a cat's, and a rabbit's temperature, and I know what questions my grandmother will ask when we call. So we might as well take her temp now. You're wasting time— time Chewie may not have. I hate to tell you, but rabbits can become really sick and die very quickly. I can't help if you don't let me."

"Okay," I say, and I lift Cuddles up for Maggie to see.

Maggie winces a little, as if Cuddles's pain is her own.

"What?" I ask.

"You're right, she has chewed out a couple of her own stitches. And she's bleeding a little, not too much, though, I don't think. Looks like three of her stitches are still holding, and I'm sure my grandma did more than one layer of sutures. Wrap her up and hold her still."

I do as she says. Maggie seems to know what she's doing as she takes Cuddles's temperature.

"One hundred and three point five," Maggie says. She writes on a small pad of paper. "That's a little high, but let me double-check my grandma's vet reference." She flips through a binder. "Yes, normal temperature range is one hundred and one to one hundred and three degrees. Any other symptoms you've observed?"

"Just the bleeding and the stitches coming out, of course, and she's been panting—she doesn't usually pant—and she's not eating. I saw her drink a little water this morning."

"Okay, stay here and I'll get her chart, just in case my grandma wrote down any other specifics or meds or anything. Then we'll call," Maggie says before she quickly leaves the room. While she's gone I double-check the chart in the binder. She's right: 101 to 103 degrees is the normal temperature range for rabbits.

Maggie picks up the wall phone when she comes back into the room and does speed-dial with just one click.

"Right," Maggie says into the phone. Then she says loud and clear for me to hear, too, as if she is repeating what Dr. Mac is saying, "Yes, I understand. We'll apply a disinfectant to clean the incision site, let that dry, cut a butterfly bandage or two, and apply those to hold the skin together, cover it with gauze, apply gentle but firm pressure if it is still bleeding . . ." Maggie stops talking and looks at me to see if I'm listening.

I nod, though I'm not sure what a butterfly bandage is. I hope she does.

"Okay," Maggie says. "I can do all that."

All what? What is Maggie going to do?

"Gran," Maggie says, "when do you think you'll be back?"

I hold my breath and pet Cuddles while I listen. Maggie's voice is serious and confident, and she keeps looking at Cuddles as if she really cares. That gives me a bit of confidence, too.

"Okay," Maggie says, still on the phone. "Yes, there are two of us. But please come as soon as you can. And oh, is the fox cub okay? Yes, I think we can do it. Bye."

I exhale. "When can she be here?" I say.

"As soon as she can," Maggie says, looking at me very quickly, then looking away. "But it might still be an hour or more. She says we shouldn't wait, because Chewie could hurt herself even more before she can get here."

Maggie looks at me again, and this time we make eye contact and hold it. She must see how worried I am. I feel all shaky inside.

"We can do this," Maggie reassures me.

"Okay," I say. "Just tell me what to do."

Chapter Nineteen

. . . .

Maggie washes her hands again and cuts some notched triangles out of adhesive tape with sterile scissors until the remaining tape looks like butterfly shapes.

"Butterfly bandages?" I ask.

Maggie nods and tells me to hold Cuddles up carefully. I do. She applies a disinfectant solution and fans it to dry. She talks to Cuddles and me in a calm voice, and Cuddles is amazingly cooperative.

"Hold her still now," Maggie says. "Good. The wound site is cleaned, and it's time to close the gap with the temporary butterfly bandages." Maggie says aloud what she is doing, just like Dr. Mac did during Cuddles's checkup.

"I'm going to gently attach these butterfly bandages, with the larger triangle on each side of where the incision is separated," Maggie says. Cuddles tries to wiggle away and tries to kick my arm. She thumps me hard. It's good Dr. Mac trimmed her nails or she would have scratched me, too.

"This is definitely a two-person job," Maggie says.

She carefully applies one of the butterfly bandages, then the other. Then she opens a sterile gauze pad and gently holds it over the butterfly bandages. "Can you hold this in place?" she asks. I do. Maggie gets a roll of stretchy bandaging, but as soon as she has wrapped it around Cuddles's belly, it bunches up and the gauze slips. "Sorry," she says. "Let me try this again." She goes around a few times, then wraps the bandage around Cuddles's shoulder and leg to hold it in place, but Cuddles wiggles and starts biting at the bandage.

"I guess we should have kept her name, Chewie," I say.

"Okay, just hold her a minute and see if she calms down. She must be nervous after all that's happened," Maggie says. "Let me think. There's got to be a way to keep her from nipping at the stitches and bandage." Maggie looks up at me. "Any ideas?" she asks.

"She needs something stretchy, like the bandage you're using, but all one piece, not a long roll. Something like a fairly tight bunny-sized T-shirt," I say.

"Good idea," Maggie says. "Maybe a one-piece stretchy tube of some kind?" She carefully places her cupped hands around Cuddles's middle to measure how big she is, then she holds both of her rounded hands midair, fingertips and thumbs touching.

Maggie shakes her head. "I was thinking my cousin's tube top might do it, but that'd be too big. We'd have to cut it and sew it around Cuddles's belly and it'd probably still slip . . . Wait! I have an idea. I'll be right back." Maggie jogs from the room.

I pet Cuddles while I wait. "You're going to be okay, Cuddles. Maggie knows what she's doing. You're in good hands." In my own hands I can feel Cuddles's heart beating a little slower, and instead of panting she takes a sigh now and then. I nuzzle her ears, but they still feel very warm.

The kittens have been mewing in their box on the floor the whole time I've been here, and now they're getting louder and louder. They must be really hungry. I hope they're okay. Maggie was feeding the calico when I arrived. I don't know if she was just starting or finishing.

Maggie comes in with a pair of pink-and-purple-striped leggings and another big pair of scissors. She holds up one of the legs and says, "What do you think?"

"Maybe," I say, "but they look brand-new."

"Yep," Maggie says with a smile, and snips off a section of one leg. "My cousin Zoe gave these to me and I've never liked them. Pink and purple stripes? Please, that's just not me."

"Your cousin in Hollywood?" I ask, remembering her Hollywood shoes on the bus that first day.

"Yes," Maggie says. "The one and only Zoe. Now I have an excuse not to wear them," she says, stretching the cut section this way and that, holding it over Cuddles to see if it will fit. She looks at me.

"Maybe a teensy bit shorter," I say.

Maggie snips off a little more. "Uh-oh," she says. "How do we keep it from unraveling? We don't want her swallowing a bunch of threads next. Where should we put the finished edge?"

Maggie is right. It doesn't matter if the cut edge is nearer Cuddles's head or tail. Wherever it is, Cuddles is sure to try to unravel it.

"We need two finished edges," I say.

"Good thing I didn't cut this one yet," Maggie says, holding up the other leg. "What if we tuck the cut end underneath?" And that's what she does. She cuts a longer section from the other side. Then she folds the cut end underneath and measures it next to Cuddles's body.

"Great," I say. "Now how do we get it on her?"

"Over her head, I think," Maggie says. "Can you lift her front legs up?"

And we do. Like Maggie said, it is definitely a two-person job, dressing a wiggly rabbit in a fancy one-legged legging. Once it is on, I carefully cradle her like a baby while Maggie tucks the cut end of Cuddles's new bellyband back underneath and checks to be sure the gauze is still in the right spot.

"Not too tight, not too loose," Maggie says, raising her eyebrows. "What do you think?"

"I think it's going to work," I say.

I set her down on the table, and Cuddles twitches her whiskers. She turns her head, as if to look at her new outfit, then ignores it altogether and sits on her haunches. She licks her paws and begins washing her face, as if she's always worn a brightly striped coat.

"Are rabbits color blind?" I ask.

"I don't know," Maggie laughs. "But my cousin

Zoe must be. That legging looks much better on your rabbit than it would ever look on me!"

"Thanks so much, Maggie," I say. "Look. She's so much calmer now. It's as if she's forgotten she has stitches. Let's see if she'll drink or eat anything." I carefully put Cuddles back in her cage. She does a small hop, then goes right to her water bottle. The little clicking sound of her drinking from the metal spout never sounded so good.

"Okay," Maggie says, taking a deep breath. "So far, so good. Let's clean up. Then onto these hungry, noisy kittens." She tosses the towel from the exam table into a bin and begins to disinfect the table with a spray bottle and paper towels.

Maggie removes her gloves, washes her hands, and puts on a new pair. "As long as you're here, do you want to help me feed these kittens?" she asks.

"Yes," I say. I throw away the paper towels, toss my gloves, and wash my hands at the sink. As I rub my hands in the warm, soapy water, I feel as if all my worries are washing away. Maybe Sunita was right. Maggie seems okay after all. I shake my head.

"What?" Maggie says.

"Nothing," I say. I have no idea how Maggie feels about me. But she cares about animals, that's for sure. She took great care of Cuddles, and she cares about these kittens, too.

"I don't get it," Maggie says. "Do you want to help feed them or not?"

"Yes. Yes, I *said* I want to help. Why?" I ask as I reach for a clean paper towel to dry my hands. I can't bring myself to look at Maggie's face.

"Because first you say yes, then you stand there shaking your head like you don't want to help. And now you say yes again, but you are acting all weird on me," Maggie says.

I turn and look at her. "I was shaking my head because I was wondering how we got off to such a bad start. You're good with animals. I'm good with animals. We have stuff in common, so it seems like we should be able to get along. I thought you were mean at first, but . . ."

"Yeah, I thought you were a total jerk, at first, too," Maggie says.

"At first?" I say, and look right at her eyes.

"Okay, I thought you were a jerk every single day—until today, that is—so I guess I acted like a jerk, too."

"I'm sorry," I say. "I'm better around animals than I am around people."

"So I guess you need help, too?" Maggie smiles.

"What do you mean?"

"My challenge is reading," Maggie says. "That's why I have a tutor to help me. Your challenge is reading people. Maybe you could use some tutoring in that?"

"Yeah," I say. "You're right."

"Okay," Maggie says, still smiling. "What do you think these kittens want?"

"Kitty formula," I say, putting on a fresh pair of gloves.

"And what do you think I want?" Maggie asks.

"You want help with the kittens?"

"Yes, and—?"

"And you want me to not ruin any more of your school projects or be a jerk anymore?"

"Yeah, but first the kittens," Maggie says, tilting her head toward the box full of noisy little mews. "Can you get the little calico? She's the next up. I tried to feed her first, but she kept turning away from me and the bottle."

"Okay," I say to Maggie, and then I pick up the little calico from the pile of kittens. She looks smaller and weaker than the others, who are climbing all over each other, mewing loudly for food. "Come here, little girl," I say, and carefully lift her to the towel in my lap. Her head droops and her neck muscles seem weak. She is so skinny I can see her little hip bones, ribs, and backbone.

"The others are gaining weight and thriving," Maggie says. "I'm worried about her."

I test the temperature of the formula to be sure it's not too hot or too cold. But when I put the bottle near the calico's mouth, she turns away. I try to get a little formula on her tiny chin and mouth but she doesn't lick, bite, or suck. Then she shivers. I wrap her in a towel to warm her, but she keeps turning away.

Maggie watches me. "See what I mean?" she asks.

"Yes," I say, and I put her back in with her siblings to stay warm. She scoots to join them, sighing deeply when she is back in the furry pile.

I get out of the chair and sit cross-legged on the floor next to the box. "I wonder," I say, taking off my gloves, "if maybe she doesn't like the gloves or the hand soap? It must be so different from the feel and smell of her brothers and sisters. I gently slide my clean bare hands back and forth over the remaining kittens in the box, rubbing both the backs and the fronts of my hands and fingers.

"What are you doing?" Maggie says.

"I'm trying to make my hands smell more familiar to her. That might be more comforting."

I take out all but the calico and place the pile of four snuggling kittens on the towel in my lap. I rub the fronts and backs of my hands on the kittens again.

"I hope this works," I say, and I carefully place the calico on top of the four-kitten huddle. She settles in, looking warm and comfortable. I squirt a tiny bit of formula on the fur of the kitten right in front of the calico's nose and mouth. She sneezes.

"Oopsie," I say. Then she licks the milky fur of her sibling. I add another drop of formula, and she licks that, too. I try the bottle with her atop the kitten pileup and she lifts her head and begins to suck, slowly at first, then more consistently. The kitten sucks the milk down, eyes closed, her tiny milky mouth and whiskers moving as she makes little *um, um* sounds. I have to keep steadying her atop the wobbling kitten huddle, but she seems to like it there. It takes a while, and her brothers and sisters are a little dripped on by the time we are through, but she drinks most of the bottle. I put her siblings back in the box. When I pick her up to burp her on my shoulder, her belly feels nice and round. I use a wet cotton ball to make her poop, like I saw Josh and David doing. Then I gently return her to the warm comfort of her brothers and sisters. She falls right to sleep.

"How'd you know to do that?" Maggie asks.

"I didn't know," I say. "Must be beginner's luck, I guess."

I glance at Cuddles in her cage. She sits comfortably now, with her funny pink-and-purple-striped bellyband doing its job. She's sipping from her water bottle again, thank goodness. I take a deep breath as I pick up another kitten, smelling the fuzzy kitty smell and feeling the warm wiggliness.

I exhale, and my shoulders relax. I turn to look at Maggie, and I see she's watching me. I am so relieved about Cuddles and the kittens and all that's happened—and Maggie must know it. I want to look away from Maggie staring at me. But I don't. We keep eye contact with each other for a few awkward seconds longer, and it's as if we're finally seeing each other for the first time.

"Hi," Maggie says, raising her eyebrows at me and smiling.

Hi? That's odd. We've been working together this last hour and now she's saying hi? I guess Maggie knows how I feel.

"Don't you wish we could start over," I say, "and pretend that all the other stuff before today never happened? Maybe create some kind of new beginning to meeting each other?"

Maggie nods.

"Me too," I say. "Hi, Maggie. Nice to meet you."

Chapter Twenty

• • • • • • • • • • •

Dr. Mac arrives as we're feeding the last two kittens.

"Is everything okay?" she asks. "I got here as soon as I could. How's Cuddles? Oh my! What a great solution!" She laughs as she kneels down to look at Cuddles in the pink-and-purple-striped finery in her cage.

Cuddles sniffs at her parsley, then takes a tiny nibble from her apple.

"Looks like Cuddles is thinking about eating again. That's good," Dr. Mac says. "Let's not disturb her for the moment. I'll wash up, and when you finish feeding that kitten, Jules, you can take Cuddles out and I'll have a closer look at her."

"Okay," I say. I'm glad Dr. Mac is here, but I already feel like Cuddles is going to be fine.

Dr. Mac washes her hands while Maggie and I tell her what happened and how we worked together to take care of Cuddles.

I hand the kitten to Maggie to burp. I wash my hands, then bring Cuddles to the exam table once again. Dr. Mac puts her gloves on and looks Cuddles over. She listens to her heart and digestive tract with her stethoscope.

"Everything sounds good. Her breathing and heart rate are normal, and her gastrointestinal tract is functioning. That's very important for rabbits, especially after surgery."

Dr. Mac takes Cuddles's temperature again. It is now 103.

"A little high, but it's coming down," Dr. Mac says. "Now, Jules, could you please cradle her on her back with her belly exposed so I can take a look at the incision site?"

Cuddles lets me hold her, and Dr. Mac gently folds the bellyband back and takes a look. "I see, yes, Cuddles has pulled out two external sutures, but your butterfly bandages are holding nicely. The bleeding has stopped. Good teamwork, you two," she says.

Maggie smiles, and I can't help smiling, too.

"Well, we have some choices," Dr. Mac says. "We could wait and see if the butterfly bandages hold and your striped bunny pajamas keep her from chewing on her stitches. I could use a little skin adhesive to help the process along. And I could take a couple more stitches. I think the best approach is a combination of these treatments so she can rest up at home again where she'll be most comfortable."

"Will it hurt for her to have stitches again?" I ask. "Will you have to put her under a general anesthetic?"

"No, the good news is, in her first surgery I made several layers of stitches and the inside stitches are holding just fine," Dr. Mac says. "I'll just take a couple of quick stitches in this outside layer. I think the main things will be keeping her great new pj's on for a few days and monitoring her temperature while watching her closely to be sure she doesn't chew at the incision site. And making sure that she begins to eat normally. We could assist her with eating if she doesn't start soon."

"How do we do that?" I ask.

"We could feed her with a syringe. There is a special formula for herbivores. We could also give her a little bit of pain medication to make her more comfortable, and an antibiotic to make sure there is no infection. But first I think we should add a few more stitches and a little adhesive."

"Okay," I say.

"Cuddles looks pretty relaxed right now," Dr. Mac tells me. "Do you want to stay and hold her while I add the stitches and glue?"

"Yes."

I stay, and Maggie assists, handing Dr. Mac the supplies she needs.

While it's hard to look at the sharp needle as Dr. Mac gets ready to take out the first stitch, it's interesting, too. And Dr. Mac is right. She ties off the two stitches and adds some skin adhesive in no time. Cuddles stays calm and never even flinches.

"That should do it," Dr. Mac says, rolling Cuddles's striped bellyband "pajamas" back over the incision. "The inner stitches will dissolve on their own. Come back in two days for me to remove the external sutures. Watch for any signs of infection, swelling, or discharge, but I think Cuddles will be perfectly fine this time around, especially if she keeps her pj's on. Cuddles should have her appetite back in no time. But, Maggie, can you get Jules a bottle of formula and a syringe just in case?"

"Thank you, Dr. Mac," I say. "And thank you,

too, Maggie. I don't know what I would have done without you."

"I'm glad I was here to help," Maggie says.

"Speaking of helping," I say, "were you able to help the fox cub, Dr. Mac?"

"Yes, thank goodness. I was worried there for a bit."

Then she tells us all about how Sunita and Brenna found a little fox with its head stuck in a rusty car part next to the stream.

"What did you do?" I ask.

"First off, that little cub was so scared and feisty that I wore my protective Kevlar gloves and gave him a mild sedative. I muzzled him as an extra precaution. When he was sleepy and relaxed, I rubbed some olive oil from the salad at the barbecue around his neck and greased up both sides of the metal disc he was stuck in. With the little guy so relaxed, I was able to carefully slide his head back out."

"So then you let the fox go after that?" I ask.

"No," Dr. Mac says. "I checked him for injuries, and luckily he seemed fine. We notified the state wildlife authority, and Brenna's parents thought it'd be best to observe him in quarantine, at their wildlife rehabilitation center, and vaccinate him against rabies before they release him in the same area they found him. They want to be sure he is fully alert, eating, and feeling okay."

"I've never seen a fox cub," I say.

"He'll be featured in Brenna's new Save Our Streams blog and the local paper," Dr. Mac says. "She took photos, and she's writing an article about how polluting our streams with trash harms local wildlife. I'll be driving out there tomorrow morning to give the cub a quick check. If you and Maggie would like to come with me, you're welcome to tag along."

I look at Maggie to be sure it's okay with her.

"Sounds good," Maggie says. "Can you come, Jules?"

"Yes," I say. "Thanks! I'd love to see all the animals there."

"Great," says Dr. Mac. "It looks like we have another veterinarian in the making. Have you ever thought of being a Vet Volunteer, Jules?"

"Me?" I ask. I look at the floor, then I look at Cuddles, and I wish I could instantly transport Cuddles and myself straight home. I can't help remembering when Maggie told me to stay away from her and the clinic. "Well, I love animals, but you probably have enough Vet Volunteers already."

I wait for some sign from Maggie to see how she'd feel about my becoming a Vet Volunteer.

Part of me is sure that Maggie will tell her grandmother they have plenty of volunteers and don't need anyone else, especially me.

Another part, a stronger part, is focusing on positive thinking. *Please, please, please. Yes, yes, yes, I'd love to be a Vet Volunteer!*

My ears start to ring in the silent room. I finally look up to see Dr. Mac giving Maggie a puzzled look.

"Actually, we do need another Vet Volunteer, maybe two," Maggie says. "And, Gran, you should see how good Jules is with the kittens. Come on, Jules, you should be a Vet Volunteer. We could use your animal communication skills. And if you need any tutoring on people communication, I'll help you out. It's *challenging* but *fun*."

I can't believe it. I'm going to get to work with animals again, and it looks like Maggie and I will be friends after all!

"Thanks!" I say. "I would love to be a Vet Volunteer. When do I start?"

"Right now," Maggie says. "I need help cleaning up, and that little calico is mewing again already."

Maggie's right. They are mewing with hunger all over again. Dr. Mac peeks into the box of kittens. "I think we need to increase their amount of kitty formula," Dr. Mac says. "I'll leave you girls to it." She pats me on the shoulder. "I'm glad you're joining us, Jules."

"Me too," says Maggie.

I feel like doing one of Cuddles's joyous bunny leap dances and shouting, *Me too, me too, me too!* But I smile and tell Maggie "Thanks" instead. Then I join her in cleaning up. And after that we get to feed the kittens again.

Cuddles is so relaxed and happy now in her cage. She doesn't seem to mind the mewing. I'm so glad she's feeling better and has stopped biting at her stitches. Cuddles scratches one floppy ear with her hind leg then looks around, suddenly curious, as if she's surprised at her surroundings and is wondering how she got here.

And again, I think, *Me too.*

• • • • •

At dinner that night, I keep Cuddles in her cage on the floor near the table so I can keep an eye on her. I don't need to use the herbivore formula because she's been munching away all afternoon, and pooping, too. I've never been so happy to see a used litter box!

I fill everyone in on the excitement at the clinic, and they tell me all about Stream Cleanup Day, about the fox, and the mud, and the zillions of bags of trash they picked up. I'm sorry I missed it, but I'm glad I was home to take care of Cuddles and to finally make up with Maggie.

"Brenna says she's planning another stream cleanup in the summer," Josh says. "So you can come to the next one. And it's cool that they invited you to be a Vet Volunteer, Jules. I'm going to ask Dr. Mac if I can be one, too."

Sophie listens to everyone else talk, then she pipes in. "Jules, your cat was there, too."

"What cat?" Mom asks.

"Jules's back-door cat," Sophie says. "The striped one."

"Jules, did you take in a cat, too?" Mom asks. "We haven't even agreed to the rabbit yet."

"No, there was a cat hanging out by the back door for a while. I was worried about him. I haven't seen him in several days. But he's not my cat. He's a stray."

"He was there at the stream cleanup," Sophie says. "I saw him near the trees at the barbecue."

"Oh, I hope he's okay. Are you sure it was the same cat?" I ask.

Sophie nods.

"Did you see, Josh?" I ask. "Mom, Dad?" But they all just shake their heads.

"He was okay," Sophie says. "Someone gave him a hot dog."

I don't know if it was the same cat or not, but for now, I'll hope it was, and that he's doing okay. I hope he finds a safe home soon. Maybe I'll convince Josh or some of the Vet Volunteers to take a hike along the stream after school this week to see if he is still there.

Mom and Dad say they liked meeting lots of townspeople and especially liked meeting Sunita and Brenna.

Josh says, "Maggie is nice, too." He gives me a funny look. "Right, Jules?"

"Yes," I say. Josh is up to something. Best to agree. Besides, now I really do believe that Maggie is nice.

"So I was thinking, Dad, what if Jules and I help you finish cleaning up the basement? Then we could create a space to hang out with our new friends down there."

"And I could design and build a bigger space for Cuddles to hop around and get exercise," I say. "A small corral with a bunny habitat inside."

Mom smiles, and Dad agrees.

Mom reaches over and pats my hand. "While we're all being so helpful and agreeable," she says, "I think we can agree to make Cuddles a permanent part of our family—so long as everybody is careful about her cage door." She looks at Sophie.

"Yay!" Sophie says. "I promise I won't forget to latch it."

"You've done a good job with Cuddles, Jules. I'm proud of you," Mom says. "And you seem to know a lot more about rabbits than the rest of us. So now that Cuddles is part of our family, you have to tell me everything important about our new pet, okay?"

"Okay," I say. Cuddles stretches her legs out one by one in her cage. Then she discovers a corner of her cardboard floor sticking up. So of course she chews on it.

"You promise?" Mom asks.

I look at Josh and Sophie, then at Mom.

"I promise," I say.

"Great," Mom says, glancing at Cuddles, who is chewing and digging at the cardboard.

"I guess I should tell you now, then," I say.

"Tell me what?"

"That Cuddles's original name was Chewie, because all rabbits, and especially our rabbit, like to chew on things," I say.

"Oh," Mom says. "Okay. Good to know. Anything else I should know?"

"Rabbits are very social creatures," I say. "So

Cuddles might be happier in the long run if she had another rabbit to snuggle and play with."

"Two rabbits?" Mom asks. "Are you suggesting we get another bunny?"

"Yes," I say, and hold my breath. *Think positive, think positive*, I tell myself.

Josh says, "Cuddles might chew on less stuff if she had a companion rabbit."

Sophie nods her head enthusiastically and whispers, "Lolli, Lolli, Lolli."

"And rabbit droppings make good compost?" Mom asks me with a wink.

"Yes," I say. I jump up and give Mom a hug.

Mom hugs me back. "I do like good compost on my roses," she says with a grin.

Dad smiles. "Vibrant, healthy-looking roses will surely attract more customers to Wrenches and Roses," he says.

"Mr. Hart says Jules is a bunny whisperer," Josh says.

"A bunny whisperer?" Mom laughs. "Who could say no to a bunny whisperer?"

She gently smooths my hair back. She moves her lips close to my ear, and whispers, "Yes."

Cuddles stops chewing on the cardboard, looks around, and does a joyful little hop.

I know exactly how she feels.

Getting Fixed

By J.J. MACKENZIE, D.V.M.

WHY SHOULD YOU HAVE YOUR PET SPAYED OR NEUTERED?

Spaying (for female pets) and neutering (for male pets) are safe and effective surgeries to prevent overpopulation. Sadly, every year millions of unwanted pets are euthanized in animal care and control centers across the nation. This could be prevented by taking your cat, dog, or rabbit to your local veterinarian or humane society to have it spayed or neutered to prevent unwanted pet pregnancies. Even if your pet is well loved, cared for, and wanted, his or her offspring might end up homeless, contributing to the overpopulation of animals.

It's not just dogs and cats that need to be spayed or neutered. Rabbits reproduce so quickly that their numbers can quickly get out of hand. There are also health and behavior benefits to spaying and neutering. Spayed and neutered rabbits are often calmer and less moody, with less destructive chewing and less undesirable territorial behavior such as spraying and various aggressive behaviors. Spayed female rabbits also enjoy better health and a longer life span than unspayed adult females, due to lower incidences of various forms of cancer.

Finally, if you have more than one pet at home, they will get along better if they are all spayed or neutered.

How should you care for your pet after spay or neuter surgery?

Follow the specific advice of your veterinarian, as each pet's needs will be slightly different. The surgery site might be sore, and your pet might be slightly groggy from the anesthetic after surgery. In general, your pet will benefit from a calm, warm, and quiet environment indoors. Be very gentle with your pet, limit active exercise, and keep young children and other pets away from your pet's stomach and incision site.

Some dogs and cats are fitted with an e-collar to prevent them from licking or biting at the incision site.

Rabbits need to eat and drink soon after surgery to keep their digestive systems healthy. If your pet doesn't seem to want to eat, offer small amounts of water and food more frequently. Follow your veterinarian's advice on when, what, and how much to feed your pet, and when to call if your pet is not eating or if the incision site is not healing.

Adopt your next pet from an animal shelter.
There are so many deserving pets at your local animal shelter looking for a loving home. Help prevent euthanasia of unwanted pets by adopting your next pet from a shelter. And then, of course, be a responsible pet owner by having your new friend spayed or neutered.

More information on the benefits of spaying and neutering your pet can be found on the American Humane Association's website at:
www.americanhumane.org/animals/adoption-pet-care/caring-for-your-pet/spaying-neutering.html

Affordable, low cost, or free neuter spay resources can be found at:
www.aspca.org/pet-care/spayneuter/

http://neuterspay.org

www.spayusa.org

Join the Vet Volunteers
on another animal adventure!

Masks

Chapter One

• • • • • • • • • • •

"You'll make an awesome tiger, Sunita," Maggie tells me as we spread our art materials across her kitchen table. It's Thursday afternoon, a week before Halloween. We've decided we'd better start making costumes for the big Halloween party at the Ambler Town Center.

"Your dark eyes will look so cool through the mask," Maggie adds.

She's totally focusing on my costume now. Once Maggie sets her mind to a project, she locks in. Sometimes she reminds me of a bulldog—playful and fun, but once she sinks her teeth into something, it's awfully hard to shake her loose!

She studies me intently, working out my costume in her mind. "I've never seen a tiger with long black hair, though. Maybe we can make you an orange-striped hood to wear. Or a scarf out of tiger-striped fabric." She smiles. "Being a tiger is just perfect for you."

I'm surprised and pleased that Maggie sees me that way, but I'm not sure that being a tiger fits my personality. I think of tigers as fierce and strong. I'm more on the shy, timid side.

Being a tiger does fit with my number-one passion in life: cats. There are lots of other things I like—computers and computer games, ballet, reading (especially about animals), and collecting Ganesha statues. (Ganesha's a sweet Hindu god with a boy's body and an elephant's head.) But there's nothing I love more than cats— domestic cats, wild cats, large and small cats.

Another reason being a tiger fits me is that one home of the tiger is India, and that's where my ancestors came from. Both my mother and father are doctors who have lived in this country for many years, but we stay in touch with our Indian background.

There's a knock on the kitchen door, and Maggie opens it. David Hutchinson and Brenna

Lake come in. Brenna has a shopping bag stuffed with even more art supplies. She begins adding them to the pile of materials we've already loaded onto the table.

"Are you going to be a horse for Halloween?" I ask David. He's wild about horses.

He shakes his head. "A vampire. I vant to suck your blood!"

"He can't figure out how to make a horse mask," Brenna adds.

"I could too!" David objects. "I just think being a horse would be sort of geeky."

"Mucho geeky," Maggie agrees.

"What will you be?" I ask her.

"A vet, of course," Maggie replies.

"You don't need a mask for that," Brenna says.

"Yes, you do—a surgical mask. Gran has a ton of them in the supply cabinet," Maggie says.

"That's too easy. No fair," Brenna says. "I want to be something unusual—maybe a unicorn. Is that too babyish? I don't know. I still have to think about it."

Dr. Mac comes in and runs her hand through her short white hair as she surveys all our stuff—colored paper, yarn, glue, markers, beads and buttons, paints, pipe cleaners, and stickers. "Wow!" she says. "What's the big project?"

Dr. Mac is Dr. J.J. MacKenzie, veterinarian extraordinaire. She lives in a big brick house with Maggie. Although Dr. Mac is Maggie's grandmother, she's so full of energy that she doesn't seem like a regular grandmother to me.

Dr. Mac and Maggie live with lots of animals. Besides their cat, Socrates, and their dog, Sherlock Holmes, they have a house full of animal patients. That's because Dr. Mac runs Dr. Mac's Place Veterinary Clinic right here, attached to her own house. She treats any animals that come through the door—pets, strays, and even wild animals. People who bring in strays or wild animals pay her what they can or sometimes nothing at all.

I volunteer at Dr. Mac's Place, along with Maggie, David, and Brenna. I love working at the clinic. In fact, my dream is to be a vet someday.

"We're making masks for the Halloween party at Town Center," Maggie tells Dr. Mac. "Do you need us, Gran?"

Dr. Mac shakes her head. "So far it's been a slow morning. If something comes up, I'll holler," she says as she leaves the kitchen.

"Guess who I saw this morning?" Brenna asks as she redoes the elastic at the end of her long brown braid. She continues without waiting for an answer. "As I was coming here, I saw the woman who just moved into that big old converted barn down the road."

"Does she have any kids?" David asks.

Brenna shrugs her slim shoulders. "I didn't see any," she answers. "My mom heard that she's some kind of artist."

"That barn would be great for a studio," I say. "It's so big, and the last owners put in skylights."

"I saw the woman at the market," Maggie says, brushing her red hair out of her eyes. "She was wearing all black, and she has wild gray hair that makes her look like a witch!"

"Oh, my gosh!" Brenna cries. "Listen to this! When I saw her, she was pulling a big black kettle out of the back of her station wagon!"

"Oh, man, she's a witch for sure!" David says, his eyes lighting up.

Brenna wraps her arms around herself and shivers. "Whoa—a witch! And just in time for Halloween! Cool!"

"I can picture her with the black kettle," David

says. "Bubble, bubble, toil and trouble!" He mimics a cackling witch voice, pretending to stir an imaginary potion.

As David does his witch act, a black-and-white tuxedo cat strolls in. It's my cat, Mittens. I brought her with me this morning, because at my house repairmen are fixing our front steps, and all the hammering was scaring her. Mittens jumps up onto the table, and I scratch her between the ears. "Hi, honey," I murmur.

Before she was mine, Mittens was a stray. I first saw her one day when she came wandering around the clinic.

"Let's go check out the witch," David says. "I've never seen a real one."

"Oh, come on!" I say, laughing. "You don't really think she's a witch!"

"You never know," David says in a low, creepy voice, his eyes darting mysteriously from side to side. "At Halloween, anything is possible."

"David, you're so weird," I tease.

"I think there might really be such things as witches," Brenna says. "They can do good stuff, too."

"Yeah," Maggie agrees. "I mean, people have

believed in them for so long. Could people be totally wrong?"

"Sure they could be wrong!" I argue. "People used to think the earth was flat, and that the sun revolved around the earth, and all sorts of crazy things."

"I heard a story once," David begins in a spooky tone. "During the Salem witch trials, a woman was hanged for being a witch. But as they put the noose around her neck, she put this horrible curse on the people. She swore she would dance on their graves.

"Every year on the anniversary of her death, footprints appeared on the graves of anyone who had watched the witch get hanged. When people tried to wipe away the footprints, their hands were covered with blood."

"Ew!" Brenna cries with a shiver.

"Creepy," Maggie agrees.

I smile and roll my eyes. Spooky stuff like witches, ghosts, and ancient curses are fun at Halloween, but they're not for real. I'll take scientific explanations every time.

Mittens begins batting markers across the table. One of the markers rolls off and falls to the floor. As I bend to pick it up, Mittens starts chewing on a button. I pull it away from her. My cat has been known to eat strange things.

She pounces on my hand with her claws sheathed. "OK! OK! I get the message," I say to her. I pull a length of thick orange yarn out of its skein and cut it off. I dangle the yarn in front of Mittens. "Here you go, Mittens—catch this!"

I reach high and jiggle the yarn. Mittens rises on her back legs and swings her paws at it.

"Go on! Catch it!" I coax, pulling the yarn just out of her reach. "You can get it, Mittens." I lower the yarn just a bit so she can have the satisfaction of capturing it.

We laugh as Mittens pounces ferociously. She reminds me of a lioness, hunting out on the savanna. She snatches the whole piece of yarn out of my hand and then sits on it, protecting her prize.

"Good job!" we praise her, clapping. "Way to go!"

I stroke my cat's silky fur. I'd wanted a cat for so long before my mother finally gave in. At first, she had a million excuses—cats shed, cats tear up the furniture, and so on. When she finally let me have Mittens, it was the happiest day of my life.

I named my cat Mittens because she looks like she's wearing two little white mittens on her front paws.

I've never met a more affectionate cat. She's always nuzzling me and giving me scratchy little love-kiss licks. I return those with a kiss on her furry forehead.

David cuts a piece of white cardboard into the shape of a face. He cuts out the eyeholes, then a slit for the mouth. "Should I draw the fangs or make them with clay?" he wonders aloud.

Suddenly there's a loud bang from outside, as if something heavy has just fallen. Some animal makes a screechy, screaming sound. The howl becomes more high-pitched.

"That is definitely a cat!" I say—a very upset, angry, threatening cat.

We jump up and rush to the door. It sounds like a cat fight, but I can hear only one cat screaming. I get to the door first and pull it open, but before I can step out, Maggie grabs my shoulder, holding me back. "Look out!" she cries as a black blur streaks by my feet.